"Maybe my coming here was a mistake."

Arden was surprised by the plea for reassurance in Rachel's statement.

"*Neh.* It wasn't a mistake." Upon seeing the fragile vulnerability in Rachel's eyes, Arden's heart ballooned with compassion. "Trust me, the community will *kumme* to help Ivan."

"In that case, I'd better keep dessert and tea on hand," Rachel said, smiling once again.

"Does that mean we can't have a slice of that pie over there?"

"Of course it doesn't. And since Ivan has no appetite, you and I might as well have large pieces."

Supping with Rachel after a hard day's work, encouraging her and discussing Ivan's care as if he were, well, not a child, but *like* a child, felt... It felt like how Arden always imagined it would feel if he had a family of his own. Which was probably why, half an hour later as he directed his horse toward home, Arden's stomach was full but he couldn't shake the aching emptiness he felt inside.

She is going back, so I'd better not get too accustomed to her company, as pleasant as it's turning out to be.

Carrie Lighte lives in Massachusetts next door to a Mennonite farming family, and she frequently spots deer, foxes, fisher cats, coyotes and turkeys in her backyard. Having enjoyed traveling to several Amish communities in the eastern United States, she looks forward to visiting settlements in the western states and in Canada. When she's not reading, writing or researching, Carrie likes to hike, kayak, bake and play word games.

Books by Carrie Lighte

Love Inspired

Amish of Serenity Ridge

Courting the Amish Nanny
The Amish Nurse's Suitor

Amish Country Courtships

Amish Triplets for Christmas
Anna's Forgotten Fiancé
An Amish Holiday Wedding
Minding the Amish Baby
Her New Amish Family
Her Amish Holiday Suitor

Visit the Author Profile page at Harlequin.com.

The Amish
Nurse's Suitor

Carrie Lighte

LOVE INSPIRED
INSPIRATIONAL ROMANCE

LOVE INSPIRED®

INSPIRATIONAL ROMANCE

Recycling programs
for this product may
not exist in your area.

ISBN-13: 978-1-335-48806-0

The Amish Nurse's Suitor

Copyright © 2020 by Carrie Lighte

This edition published by arrangement with Harlequin Books S.A.

For questions and comments about the quality of this book,
please contact us at CustomerService@Harlequin.com.

Love Inspired
22 Adelaide St. West, 40th Floor
Toronto, Ontario M5H 4E3, Canada
www.Harlequin.com

Printed in U.S.A.

But the wisdom that is from above is first pure, then peaceable, gentle, and easy to be intreated, full of mercy and good fruits, without partiality, and without hypocrisy.
—*James* 3:17

For the kind *Englischers* and Amish people of Unity, Maine, who enthusiastically helped me with my research, and with thanks to my brother for "talking shop" about lumber.

Chapter One

"Toby probably didn't think I was ambitious or smart enough for him," Rachel Blank told her roommate, Meg.

It had been nearly two weeks since her boyfriend had broken up with her—the same amount of time Meg had been away on vacation—and by this point Rachel was more angry than sad.

"Not ambitious or smart enough?" Meg's voice rose with incredulity. "What else would he call someone who started out with an eighth-grade education but later earned her GED, her BSN, and is going to school to become a nurse practitioner?"

"He doesn't know I applied to the MSN program, and I haven't actually been accepted into it yet, either," Rachel protested feebly. Meg didn't seem to hear. She was pacing in front of the sofa, counting on her fingers as she reeled off Rachel's accomplishments.

"You've learned to drive, you've learned to swim and you've mastered more technology than many people who've grown up surrounded by it. Not to mention you're fluent in three languages—English, German and *Deitsch*. If the tables were turned, Dr. Toby Grand wouldn't last a week living like an Amish person."

Rachel appreciated her roommate's impassioned defense of her, but she was uncomfortable with her praise. When she left her Amish community and family ten years ago, they'd accused Rachel of *hochmut*. High-mindedness. Pride. They said her pursuit of higher education was, among other things, an attempt to draw attention to herself. The implication stung so deeply that even now at twenty-eight she resisted it when anyone pointed out her accomplishments. Which, fortunately for her, Toby had rarely done. Instead, he'd pushed her to reach more difficult goals, which was one of the reasons Rachel hadn't told him she'd applied to an MSN program; she didn't want to disappoint him if she was rejected.

"Well, those weren't his exact words. But even if they were, I suppose I understand why he wants to date Brianna. She's a doctor, too. I'm only a nurse."

"*Only* a nurse?" Meg stopped pacing and thrust her hands on her hips. Meg was also a nurse, although she worked in a hospital, whereas Rachel worked at a clinic in the suburbs.

"*Neh, neh, neh*, I'm not saying *I* think nurses are inferior." Rachel sometimes accidentally reverted to *Deitsch* when she was flustered. "That's what *Toby* thinks. He says Brianna has more in common with him than I do."

"Yeah. They're both sneaks."

Toby had only broken up with Rachel *after* he'd been on several dates with Brianna, the practice's newly hired doctor. That's what vexed Rachel most—the betrayal.

"They probably thought it would be easy to pull one

over on the naive Amish girl. And they were right. I had no idea Toby and Brianna had been seeing each other."

"That's not because of your Amish background. It's because you're an honest person who extended trust to someone you loved."

Did I love Toby? Rachel asked herself. During the ten months of their relationship, she'd definitely developed stronger feelings for him than for any man she'd dated, and she'd thought those feelings were reciprocated. In fact, when Toby came over to break up with her, his expression had been so somber she'd suspected he was about to propose. The ironic thing was, she wasn't sure how she would have answered. Afterward, as devastated as she was by the circumstances of their breakup, a small part of her felt relieved he hadn't asked her to marry him.

Meg shook a finger at Rachel. "You'd better not ever take him back."

"I doubt he'd ever want to *come* back, but no, I absolutely wouldn't go out with him again. He crossed a line that can't be uncrossed," Rachel assured her friend. "With God's grace I'll forgive him eventually, but right now, it's hard enough to even *look* at him at work."

Regardless, each day she held her head high and made a point to greet him and Brianna with a big smile, knowing the kind of office rumors that would erupt if she gave any indication of how deceived or miffed she really felt. She wouldn't give her coworkers the satisfaction. *Maybe I have more* hochmut *than I care to admit*, she mused.

"You should take a vacation. Maybe go to Maine for a few days…"

Rachel recognized Meg was hinting she should visit

her family. Her roommate was one of the few people Rachel had confided in about how much she missed them sometimes. But missing them and visiting them were two different matters. Rachel hadn't been baptized into the Amish church before she left for the *Englisch* world, so she wasn't in the *Bann*, but in some ways, she felt like she might as well have been.

Both of her parents had passed away before she left her Amish community in Serenity Ridge, Maine. Rachel had two older married brothers, Colin and Albert, and one younger brother, Ivan, a bachelor. Initially her family members had been understandably hurt, disappointed and angry when Rachel told them she was moving to Massachusetts to pursue an education in nursing. Colin's wife, Hadassah, claimed she spoke for the entire family when she told Rachel unless and until she returned to Serenity Ridge and the Amish for good, she shouldn't bother to return at all.

Rachel thought in time they'd come to accept her decision even if they disagreed with it. Yet her monthly letters went unanswered, except by her youngest brother, Ivan, who wrote twice a year—at Christmas and Easter. But Easter had passed a week ago without a note from him, either. She was beginning to accept that although she'd never stop praying for or loving her family, the same might not be true for them.

"I've had enough rejection for the time being."

"Then you should go somewhere fun." Meg snapped her fingers. "A Christian singles' cruise! Wouldn't Toby and the people at work faint if you came back from the Bahamas with a new boyfriend? That would shatter their assumptions about you."

As well as Rachel had adapted to the *Englisch* lifestyle, she couldn't picture herself going on a singles' cruise, even if she were desperate to meet a man, which she most definitely was not. If she'd made it through the heartache of leaving her family behind at eighteen, she'd make it through life without a boyfriend at twenty-eight. Her faith, career and friendships were all she needed to be fulfilled. In fact, the breakup couldn't have come at a better time, since she'd soon have to devote herself to furthering her education. "No, I'm saving every cent I have for tuition. If I get in to the MSN program, I'll be too busy studying to have time for a relationship."

"First of all, it's not *if* you get in to the MSN program, it's *when*. Secondly, you'll be too busy for a relationship? Wow. You sound more *Englisch* than I do!"

Rachel chuckled again, but the truth was, she didn't feel particularly *Englisch*. Nor did she feel Amish. She felt…alone. No—she felt *independent*. And that suited her just fine.

Arden Esh had stacked so much mail on the little desk in the workshop the pile slid like an avalanche onto the floor. He stooped to pick up the envelopes. Sooner or later he was going to have to open them. He hoped they were bills and not customer orders; he and his business partner, Ivan Blank, needed all the sales they could get. They'd sunk every spare cent into advertising their shed-building business, and after three years of barely profiting, this spring they hoped to see an increase in revenue.

Arden couldn't imagine how, exactly, that was going to happen with him manning the shop alone. Not that money was the most important matter at the moment—

Ivan's recovery was. He'd been sick for almost two weeks, and two days ago he wound up in the hospital.

Last evening when Arden visited him there, Ivan had barely opened his eyes. Arden had chatted about the shed he'd just finished. He didn't even know if Ivan was awake until Ivan pulled aside his oxygen mask and rasped, "Would you write to Rachel? Ask her to *kumme* as soon as she can. She'll help you in the shop. Don't..." He was having difficulty breathing. "Don't tell anyone, though."

Initially, Arden had been taken aback by the request. Ivan often spoke fondly of his sister, who'd left the Amish a decade ago to become a nurse. They'd kept in touch, but Ivan had confided that his sister-in-law Hadassah made it clear Rachel wasn't welcome to visit. Arden felt a pang of guilt, aware that Ivan wouldn't have subjected his family to the tension of a reunion if he believed Arden could manage the shop—specifically, the paperwork—by himself. Long ago the two men had come to an unspoken understanding about the division of their responsibilities. For lack of a better expression, in many ways Ivan was the brains of the operation and Arden was the brawn.

Considering Ivan's family hadn't supported his business venture from the beginning, Arden understood why Ivan was reluctant to ask one of his brothers for help with administrative tasks during his illness. Ivan said Rachel was a very intelligent, capable woman who'd often expressed her desire to see him again. But her presence would undoubtedly create controversy. Regardless, Ivan was the one who had founded the business, so even though Arden had eventually become an equal partner in it, he deferred to Ivan's judgment in the matter.

Now, as Arden searched the desk for Ivan's address book, a disturbing possibility occurred to him: Ivan wanted Rachel to visit because he believed he was dying and wanted to say goodbye. The very thought stopped Arden cold. He immediately dropped to his knees. *Dear Gott, if it's Your will, please heal Ivan. Give those caring for him wisdom and fill him with a sense of Your loving presence. Amen.* Then, knowing no request was too small or too big for the Lord, he added, *And please help me find that address book.*

He stood, brushed the knees of his trousers and lifted a stack of catalogs. Beneath them was a blank piece of paper with the salutation *Dear Rachel* scrawled at the top, and beneath the stationery was an addressed, stamped envelope. Ivan must have begun writing his annual Easter letter to his sister—he was nothing if not conscientious—but he had been too sick to finish it. Silently thanking the Lord for the unexpected way He'd answered his prayer, Arden cleared a space at the desk, sat down and picked up a pen.

As he stared at the blank page, his hairline beaded with perspiration and his tongue tasted sour. This was why Ivan handled virtually all of the paperwork while Arden compensated by doing whatever heavy lifting Ivan's slighter frame couldn't handle. It wasn't that Arden *couldn't* read or write—it was that it took him so painfully long because the letters often seemed to jump around and didn't make any sense. It had been that way for as long as he could remember, and although his schoolteacher had thought he'd outgrow it if he practiced more or tried harder, he never did. The only thing more daunting to Arden than a page filled with text was a completely blank sheet of paper. He threw down the pen and strode to the other side of the workshop to pick up a hammer. Now *this* was a tool he could use as deftly as if it were an extension of his own arm.

How could Ivan ask me to write to his sister, of all people? When Ivan spoke of Rachel, there was nothing except admiration and affection in his voice. But there were others in Serenity Ridge whose opinions of Rachel weren't as high; they indicated she thought herself a tad superior to those in her family and community. If their assessment of her character was correct, Arden expected she'd have a good laugh about the "ignorant" Amish man's spelling.

No, Arden couldn't write to her. As he drove a nail into a floor joist, he thought, *If I can find that address book, I'll look up her phone number and call her instead.* But by the end of the day, he'd turned the desk upside down and inside out and come up empty-handed. He was going to have to face the page. Maybe his mother or his younger sister, Grace, would proofread the letter. *No, I can't show it to them. Ivan said not to tell anyone else he wants Rachel to* kumme.

He took a deep breath and stared at the stationery. What should he say? "Your brother is in the hospital with pneumonia"? He doubted he could get the spelling right for the word *hospital*, much less *pneumonia*. One thing he'd learned over the years—when it came to writing, reading and speaking, shorter was better. With his hand shaking as much as if he'd just downed four cups of coffee, Arden positioned his pen under the words *Dear Rachel* and inscribed:

Your brother is very ill. Please come soon if you can.
Signed,
Arden Esh

Arden chewed the end of the pen. Had he spelled *signed* correctly? Words that were spelled differently than they sounded gave him the most trouble. But if he crossed it out, it would look too messy and he'd have to start over with a new sheet. The prospect made him shudder. He folded the paper in quarters, slid it into the envelope and carried it to the mailbox at the end of the long driveway.

Even though he was doing exactly what Ivan had asked him to do, Arden couldn't escape the feeling he was letting him down. If only Arden didn't have such difficulty with words, he could take care of the paperwork himself. Of course, if Arden didn't have such trouble with words, he never would have moved to Maine, because he would have been able to get through an interview and secure a factory job in Indiana. *I'd probably be married with two or three* kinner *by now, too.*

Arden was glad Serenity Ridge's Amish community was small with very few single women; it gave him a plausible excuse for not courting anyone. The couple of times he'd walked out with anyone in Indiana had been utterly discouraging. His verbal difficulties had made him more nervous than usual, rendering him speechless. The women must have construed his silence as disinterest or else thought he was stupid, because none of them walked out with him for long.

It's just as well, he consoled himself, remembering. *Courting is intended to lead to marriage, and marriage leads to* bobblin. Arden's father had suffered the same problem as Arden, but to a lesser degree. Assuming the issue was hereditary, Arden couldn't knowingly subject his offspring to a lifetime of the kind of shame, frustration and struggles he'd faced. He'd decided years ago not to torment himself—or disappoint a woman—by engaging in courtship when he knew it wouldn't progress to marriage.

Just because I can't be a husband or a daed *doesn't mean I'm not responsible for making the most of the opportunities* Gott *has given me, including supporting my* schweschder *and* mamm, he thought. *So I've got to do whatever it takes to keep the business afloat during Ivan's illness.* Even if that meant working side by side with Ivan's condescending *Englisch* sister.

"You got in so late last night I didn't get to ask how Ivan is," his sister said to Arden later over a supper of *bottboi*, an Amish version of pot pie made with chicken and noodles.

"He was resting well." Arden didn't want to worry Grace. She had her hands full taking care of their mother, Oneita, who was experiencing a severe flare of lupus symptoms.

As supportive as their community in Maine was, Arden frequently regretted he'd had to relocate his mother and sister so far from their beloved district in Indiana. Since he couldn't get a factory job and there was a surplus of carpenters in the area, Arden had moved to Maine some three years ago when he heard about the shed-building opportunity with Ivan. Shortly afterward, Arden's father had died, so Arden had brought his mother and sister out to live in Serenity Ridge, as well.

"I wish I could visit him," Grace said. "So he knows how much I—*we*—care about him."

Arden appreciated his sister's sentiment, but she couldn't leave their mother alone in her current condition. Even if Grace wanted to go to the hospital after Arden returned home for the evening, cab fare was an expense they could scarcely afford. "I told him you were praying."

"*Jah*, but I want to do something tangible, the way other people do for *Mamm* when she's ill. Maybe I could make meals to put in his freezer for when he comes home."

"He'd probably *wilkom* that," Arden agreed. He forced himself to dismiss his niggling fear about Ivan's health declining even further.

"I can clean the *haus* for him, too. Make sure he has fresh sheets and do the dusting and window washing. I'll do it when Jaala comes over to visit *Mamm* tomorrow."

"That's a *wunderbaar* idea." Arden figured even if Ivan didn't get out of the hospital for a while, at least Ivan's sister would appreciate arriving to a clean house.

On Thursday evening Rachel described to Meg how mortified she'd been when she walked in on Brianna and Toby kissing in the break room that day. She'd quickly grabbed her lunch from the fridge and eaten it in her car, which would have been enjoyable because the weather was so warm, but her allergies caused her eyes and nose to run. When she returned to the office, her coworkers assumed she'd been crying over Toby and Brianna's break-room canoodling.

"Unbelievable," Meg empathized. "But it might brighten your day to know you have mail on the hall table."

Was it news from the university? Even though she knew it was immature, Rachel couldn't wait until Toby found out she'd been accepted into the program. Countless times since he'd broken up with her she'd imagined his stunned expression when she oh-so-casually told her coworkers she was resigning to get her MSN... Unless she *didn't* get into the program. At the possibility, Rachel's stomach twisted into a knot. Then she remembered she would receive the decision via email, not regular post. When she retrieved the letter, she noticed the address was written in her brother's familiar cursive.

"It's from Ivan!" she announced, chagrined that she'd doubted he wanted to keep in touch. But when she scanned the letter, her knees wobbled and she dropped into a chair. "Oh *neh*."

"What is it? What's wrong?"

Rachel extended the paper to her roommate. "My *bruder* is sick."

It only took a second for Meg to read the message. "This is upsetting, but I'm sure everything's going to be okay," she said, giving Rachel a hug. "C'mon, I'll help you pack so you'll be ready to go first thing in the morning."

Following her, Rachel fretted, "Ivan's so ill he couldn't even write to me himself. I can't believe my other brothers didn't contact me sooner. What if he's dying? What if I'm too late?"

Meg twirled around and placed her hands firmly on Rachel's shoulders. "You won't know how sick Ivan is until you get there. It's not helpful to imagine the worst-case scenario."

"That's true," Rachel hesitantly concurred.

Meg pulled a suitcase from the closet and opened it

across the bed. "Do you think you'll be calm enough to drive? If you need me to take you, I will."

Meg was the closest person Rachel had to a sister and she loved her for her generosity and support, but Rachel knew she'd used the last of her PTO to go on vacation. "Thanks, but I'll be fine. And you're right—I can't let my imagination get the best of me."

But as she lay awake in bed an hour later, Rachel's apprehension about Ivan's health returned. *Very ill,* the note had said, but what did that mean? Ivan always described his business partner in glowing terms, but Arden must have been quite dense not to have provided more details. Or maybe he was deliberately terse; it was possible he only wrote the note because Ivan pressed him to write it since no one else would. Either way, Rachel hoped their paths wouldn't cross too often while she was in Serenity Ridge. After Toby broke up with her, Rachel had made up her mind to stay as far away from thoughtless, insensitive men like him as she could.

Leaving early the next morning, Rachel prayed during most of the three-and-a-half-hour drive from Boston to Maine, but the closer she got to Serenity Ridge, the queasier she became. Not only was she anxious about Ivan's health, but she was uneasy about the reception she'd get from her family. As she crested the long hill leading to her old home—the house Ivan, the youngest boy in their family, had inherited according to their Amish tradition—her hands were clammy on the steering wheel. Would she find her brothers in the yard? Maybe her sisters-in-law would be in the kitchen, making soup for Ivan.

On first glance she didn't spot any buggies when

she pulled up in the driveway, nor did she see anyone as she crossed the lawn and climbed the porch stairs. It seemed strange to knock on the door of the place she'd once called home, but Rachel rapped twice and waited, stealing a look around the front yard. When no one came, she knocked again, louder. No response. Like most of the Amish in Serenity Ridge, the Blanks didn't lock their doors, so Rachel pushed it open.

"Ivan? Hello?" She timidly crossed the threshold. "Anyone home?"

She passed through the kitchen and stuck her head into the living room—no one was there, either. Then she went upstairs, announcing her presence. If her brother was sleeping, she didn't want to startle him by bursting into his room. "Ivan, it's me, Rachel."

His room was empty, the bed made. *This was where Ivan slept as a boy—now that he has his choice of rooms, he probably moved into the bigger one at the end of the hall.* But he wasn't there, either. As she darted to check the other two bedrooms, Rachel noticed the unmistakable scent of vinegar—someone had recently washed the windows. In fact, the entire house had been scrubbed clean. It was immaculate, as if no one had ever lived there. That could only mean one thing—the women from church had cleaned Ivan's house, as was their practice when someone died. It was a way of caring for the family of the bereaved, who were expected to host the community after a funeral. Rachel collapsed onto the bed in her old room and sobbed, her worst fear realized: she was too late.

Arden stopped hammering. He thought he'd heard a vehicle pull up the lane, so he waited for the customer to enter the workshop. When no one did, he resumed pounding until a couple of moments later, when he realized maybe it was Ivan's sister who had arrived. He set his hammer down and blew a curly lock of hair from his forehead. Meeting new people, especially *Englischers*, wasn't something he relished or excelled at doing.

Outside he noticed the little green sedan had Massachusetts plates, so Arden ambled slowly toward the house and pushed open the door. Taking a deep breath, he mentally prepared to say hello, but Rachel wasn't in the kitchen. Figuring she was in the bathroom, he waited for her to come out, but after a few minutes he concluded she wasn't in there, either.

"Hello?" he called as he entered the living room. "Hello?"

There were footsteps on the staircase, and then a young, slender *Englisch* woman dressed in a long green skirt and black top appeared in the doorway of the living room. Her auburn hair hung to her shoulders in soft layers. She must have either had a cold or else she'd been crying, because she dabbed her red-rimmed nostrils with a tissue.

"Hello," she murmured, glancing up at him. She had the same broad forehead and narrow jaw as her brother, although her almond-shaped eyes were hazel instead of brown, and now that he looked into them, Arden was convinced he had indeed caught her weeping. As if an introduction were necessary, she said, "I'm Ivan's sister, Rachel Blank."

"I'm Arden Esh, the one who wrote to you. I'm your brother's business partner."

Rachel nodded solemnly. "Ivan told me about you.

He was very…" There was a catch in her voice. "He was very appreciative of your skills."

"*Denki*," Arden muttered. He wasn't used to receiving compliments from a woman, nor was he accustomed to chatting with someone who was clearly fighting back tears. Generally speaking, the Amish were less demonstrative about their emotions than the *Englisch*.

Rachel broke eye contact and took a seat on the sofa. She smoothed her skirt as she spoke. "*Denki* for writing to me. When did Ivan…how did he…"

As her chin dropped to her chest, her hair made a curtain obscuring her face, but from the way her shoulders were quivering, Arden could tell she was crying. Whenever he'd interacted with medical professionals, they came across as calm and collected, no matter how severe an injury or bleak a diagnosis, so Rachel's behavior caught him off guard.

"I'd, uh, I'd say it was about ten or twelve days ago when he came down with a bad case of bronchitis. But it turned out it wasn't really bronchitis—or maybe it started out that way, but then it developed into—" Arden paused, afraid he'd stumble over the word *pneumonia*. It was easier to describe the symptoms instead. "Each day it became more and more difficult for him to breathe. But then yesterday his condition, uh, took a turn…"

Rachel lifted her head to look at him, and Arden knew his cheeks were flushed. "It's okay. You don't have to tell me anything else right now," she said tearfully.

He thought learning that her brother was improving would have made her happier. "Do you want tea?" he suggested, hoping she didn't so he could go. "Or to lie down upstairs?"

"No, thanks. I'd rather not. Too many memories. I'll book myself into a hotel."

Arden expressed his surprise. "Oh. I think Ivan hoped you'd stay here. You know, to care for the animals and keep an eye on the *haus*. But I can continue doing that if you'd rather not."

She slowly shook her head. "No. If that's what Ivan wanted, I'll honor his request. It's only for a few days. I imagine the livestock will go to Colin or Albert after the funeral, right?"

"The funeral? Whose funeral?"

Rachel's mouth gnarled into a frown. "Whose do you think? *Ivan's* funeral," she sobbed.

The room tilted as it usually did when he panicked, and Arden couldn't find the words fast enough to explain. He couldn't find them at *all*, not with Rachel bawling into her hands like that, her shoulders convulsing, and Arden knowing he was somehow the cause of her distress.

"Your—your—your *bruder* isn't ha-having a funeral," he stuttered. Then he clarified bluntly, "Ivan's not dead."

Rachel's shoulders lifted and dropped a few more times before she turned her head toward him, still bent forward, her arms crossed against her chest, her face red. "What did you say?"

"Ivan's not dead. He's in the hospital. He has pneu-pneu-pneum…" The word wouldn't come out, but it didn't matter anyway. Rachel shot from the room and within seconds Arden heard her retching in the bathroom. He pushed his hand through his hair and circled the braided rug, wondering whether he should check on her.

Before he could decide, she flew back into the room, her eyes blazing. "What is *wrong* with you?"

Humiliation scalded Arden's face and reduced him to being a schoolchild at the chalkboard again, struggling to solve what should have been a simple word problem. *What is wrong with me* was a question he'd asked himself countless times since then, and he still didn't know the answer.

"How could you send me a note like that? How could you stand there and tell me about my *bruder* fighting to breathe and his condition taking a turn, especially since I came here to find the house empty and immaculate? You had to have known I thought Ivan died!" She gasped and then pressed a hand against her lips and the other against her heart, as if to quiet them both.

She was right; the misunderstanding *was* his fault. He should have expressed himself better. He had no defense; all he could do was apologize. "I'm sorry. It was a miscom-commun-communication."

"That's putting it mildly," Rachel uttered, but the fight had gone out of her voice, and her shoulders drooped, too. She wiped beneath her eyes and stated more than asked, "Ivan's still alive?"

"Jah. He's in the hospital, but he's getting better."

Rachel sniffed, nodding. Then she said, "I think I need a glass of water."

"I'll get it." Arden was relieved to have an excuse to leave the room. When he returned, Rachel was perched in a straight-backed chair on the opposite side of the coffee table. He handed her the glass and reluctantly lowered himself onto the sofa. After apologizing again, he told her he'd be too busy filling orders to manage the administrative side of their business, which was why Ivan had requested Rachel come to Serenity Ridge.

"I'm surprised he didn't ask Colin or Albert or their wives. Or someone else from the district."

"Our community is still relatively small, and spring is planting season. Your brother Albert and his wife went to Ontario because her mother is sick. As for Colin, his roofing business picks up at this time of year, too. Ivan didn't ask Hadassah because she's, uh…"

"Too bossy?"

Arden suppressed a chuckle. Ivan *had* mentioned Hadassah's habit of giving him unsolicited advice, but that wasn't the only reason he hesitated to involve her in their business. "She's, uh, with child. Twins, apparently. She tires easily."

"Oh, so Ivan didn't have any choice other than to ask me."

"*Neh, neh.* That's not why. I'm sure it's because of how *schmaert* and competent you are." His response brought a sliver of a smile to Rachel's lips.

"I'm glad to help for as long as I'm needed," she replied.

"Ivan will be relieved to hear that," Arden said. *But not half as relieved as I'll be when it's time for you to go.*

Sitting across from Rachel with his large hands resting on his knees as he squeezed his legs into the space between the sofa and the coffee table, Arden appeared as tentative as a young boy who'd just been scolded and was afraid to move for fear of further punishment. Pale blue eyes and a mass of curly, dirty-blond hair contributed to his youthful appearance, but given his manly

physique and the faint crinkle of skin at the corners
of his eyes, Rachel figured he was about thirty-one
or thirty-two years old. His thick, level brows emphasized the rectangular shape of his forehead, but it was
his mouth that captured her attention—she wondered
what it would take to put a smile on those broad lips.

*I suppose it's my fault he looks so grim. It's possible
I overreacted.* Before Rachel could think of a way to
lighten the mood, an approaching vehicle interrupted
the silence.

Rising, Arden said, "That might be a delivery. I
should get back to the workshop."

Rachel stood, too, subconsciously estimating Arden's height at six-one or six-two as she walked him
to the door. She watched as he hurried down the stairs
and across the driveway. She knew men in the *Englisch*
world who spent hours at the gym trying to develop a
similar physique: small waist, broad shoulders and bi-
ceps so muscular she could see their outline beneath his
cobalt-blue cotton shirt. That must have been what Ivan
meant when he jokingly wrote one of Arden's strengths
was his strength, which was a good thing, because one
of Ivan's weaknesses was his weakness.

My poor bruder *is probably weaker than ever right
now.* Keenly aware that pneumonia severe enough to be
hospitalized sometimes could be a touch-and-go condition, Rachel thanked the Lord that Ivan was still alive
and after ten years, she was finally about to see him
again.

Chapter Two

After bringing her suitcase in from the car, Rachel washed her face and took her cell phone out of her purse. The low-battery warning flashed, so she quickly texted Meg—Rachel had promised to let her know when she arrived—and made a mental note to pick up a phone charger she could use in her car, since there was no electricity in the house. She was about to get back in her car when she realized she hadn't asked which hospital Ivan was in, nor had Arden volunteered the information. *I wonder if there's much information that he ever volunteers,* she mused as she walked toward the backyard. *He might not be as thoughtless as I suspected he was, but he's definitely a man of few words.*

Remembering how Ivan had written he'd converted the barn into a workshop and the smaller workshop into a stable, Rachel thought back to when her family moved to Maine from Ohio some twenty years ago. Her father had built a barn big enough for their milk cows, horses, buggy and equipment. He'd also constructed a small workshop for personal use. He and his cousin started a metal roofing supply and installation business, but because the cousin's land was more centrally located to the *Englisch* community, their main workshop was housed on his property, which Colin now owned. Rachel's brother Albert was a partner in the business, too.

Ivan was the only one who hadn't taken up the family trade. He had a deeply rooted fear of heights, a fear Colin and Albert had reportedly accommodated by assigning Ivan administrative responsibilities in the shop. Although he was adept at accounting and customer service, Ivan soon grew restless. Rachel understood perfectly why building sheds was a better fit for his blend of carpentry skills and temperament, but Colin and Albert undoubtedly believed Ivan should have derived satisfaction from participating in the family business. Although he'd never written about any conflict directly, Rachel could imagine Ivan's professional choice was met with nearly as much family opposition as Rachel's decision to leave the Amish.

Entering the barn through a new side door labeled Customer Entrance, Rachel surveyed the workshop, impressed by how bright and tidy the spacious interior was. Four small buildings in various stages of construction were situated in separate quarters of the work area. Metal shelving held an assortment of equipment, tools and other supplies along the periphery of the room on one side. A substantial quantity of lumber was stacked in racks near the wall on the other two sides, and what appeared to be recently installed overhead doors ran the length of the fourth wall. Rachel paused and inhaled the piney scent.

Because Arden wasn't in sight and the hum of the nearby generator was so loud, she shouted his name. Hunched over, he emerged from a little wooden structure that looked more like an oversize dollhouse than a shed. When he straightened to his full height beside it, he reminded her of an illustration of a giant in a children's book, and she giggled.

"If that's the size of the house, I can only imagine how tiny its shed is."

Arden glowered. "It's a playhouse for an *Englischer*'s eight-year-old *dochder*. It might seem frivolous to you, but it's what the customer ordered and we need the business."

Rachel instantly regretted her joke. She wasn't mocking his work—with its scalloped eaves and miniature window boxes, the tiny house was beautifully designed. It took her by surprise to see him come out of it, that's all. "I forgot to ask which hospital Ivan is at, the one in Waterville or in Pittsfield?"

"Neither. It's the one in Belridge."

"Belridge? That must be new since I lived here. Can you tell me how to get there?"

Arden squinted and rubbed his neck as if it was giving him a headache. "You take 202 through Unity."

"And then?" she prompted.

"Don't you have PSG?"

Finding it ironic an Amish person would suggest she use technology, Rachel chuckled. "You mean GPS?"

"*Jah*. You should use that. It's more accurate, and I'm busy."

"Oh, okay," Rachel replied, but Arden had already ducked back into the playhouse. His abrupt departure made her feel foolish. It could have been he was stressed out about his workload, but she got the feeling he was annoyed with her for joking around.

At the end of the driveway, Rachel let the car's engine run idle. If she turned right, the same way she came in, she'd head toward the highway. If she turned left, she'd travel directly past Colin's property. Colin or Hadassah surely would be able to tell Rachel how to get to the hospital, assuming they were home and willing to talk to her. *But if they give me the cold shoulder, I might end up blubbering again, and I need to stay as upbeat as I can before visiting Ivan.* Without further hesitation, Rachel turned right. If her Amish family and Ivan's coworker couldn't be counted on to give her directions, she'd just have to stop at the nearest gas station, where she'd ask an *Englisch* stranger to help her find her way.

Arden waited until he was certain Rachel had driven away before coming out of the playhouse again. He felt like such a *dummkopf* in her presence. The rumors he'd heard were proving to be more accurate than not; Rachel *was* rather smug, giggling at the way he'd botched up that acronym. As for directions to the hospital, he saw the trip in his mind's eye so clearly he could have led her there blindfolded, but *telling* her how to get there was another story. Arden might as well have tried to talk her through the Sahara Desert and back again.

What really irked him, though, was the way she'd looked down her nose at his work on the playhouse. It was one thing for her to be amused by his verbal inadequacies, but Arden took great care to produce high-quality products. Even if it seemed impractical by Amish standards, the playhouse was meaningful to the customer, Mrs. McGregor, and Arden was committed to surpassing her expectations for craftsmanship and service. Not to mention, he was dedicated to doing whatever he could, in good conscience, for the business to prosper.

And as Arden had just discovered, sometimes that meant completing customers' orders sooner than originally promised. Mrs. McGregor had come to inquire if he could finish the project the following Friday, a week ahead of schedule. Since it was the end of April and several customers wanted their sheds ready before summer, Arden was juggling other projects simultaneously. But because painting the playhouse was virtually all he needed to do before the project was completed, Arden agreed. Mrs. McGregor subsequently produced two gallons of her daughter's favorite shade of paint for Arden to use. Lovely Lavender, she'd called it. Or was it Lively Lilac? Either way, it looked purple to him.

I'll have to ask Rachel to schedule the earlier delivery, he reminded himself. Sometimes Arden kept so many details in his head he was surprised his skull didn't tilt to the side, but recording information in his brain was far easier for him than jotting it down on paper.

As he took a swig of water from his thermal cup, he heard another vehicle in the driveway—too loud to be Rachel's—and went outside. Two men jumped down from the cab of a large flatbed truck and headed his way.

The stockier one, who had the name *Bob* emblazoned on his shirt pocket, said, "The shake shingles will arrive from our Montville site on Tuesday, but as you can see, we've brought your two-by-sixes."

"That can't all be mine," Arden objected, surveying the load.

The taller, wiry guy snorted. "Funny."

Arden wasn't joking. "I didn't order that much. Our customers have been choosing pine, so we only need half as much cedar as usual. That looks like twice the amount."

"Hang on a sec." Bob retrieved a clipboard from the cab and brought it to Arden. Tapping it with his knuckle he said, "Yup. Someone named Allen put in the order. Signature's right here."

"Arden," Arden corrected the man. "That's me, but that's not the quantity I ordered."

For as much difficulty as he had with reading and writing, Arden didn't have any problem with math. Knight's was a new lumberyard; maybe they'd made a mistake. Arden and Ivan had only been contracted with them for a couple of months, so perhaps the employees were confusing theirs with an *Englisch* business.

"Your paperwork shows you did. Check for yourself—it's a photocopy of the order you placed. The note says you mailed it in." Bob handed the clipboard to Arden.

Arden distinctly recalled the afternoon he'd tried to phone in the order—the *Ordnung* allowed cell phones and solar chargers for business use—as he'd done with the previous lumberyard he and Ivan patronized. The clerk insisted he'd have to place the order online, by fax or in person, because they required a customer signature. Arden explained he didn't have a computer or fax machine and the lumberyard was too far away for his horse to get there in one day, which caused the woman to crack up. When she realized Arden was indeed Amish, she'd apologized profusely.

"You can make up an order sheet yourself. Just use the product codes from the catalog and indicate the amounts. You don't even have to write the sizes down, because we can tell exactly what you want by the codes, but don't forget to sign your name at the bottom."

Studying the sheet now, Arden's mouth went dry. It looked right to him, but then again, he misread things more often than not.

After a minute, Bob took the clipboard back. He pointed to the left of the page, "See here? This is the product code for cedar two-by-sixes. This is the amount you ordered. Here's the product code for the shake shingles, and again, you wrote the amount right beside it."

That explained it: Arden had been so concerned about accidentally transposing letters when he copied the product codes from the catalog that he'd proofread them three or four times. Unfortunately, he didn't pay as careful attention to the quantities. He must have matched the quantity of two-by-sixes with the product code for the shake shingles and vice versa. Red-faced, he admitted his error to Bob.

"We only need half as much cedar, and we'll need double the amount of shake shingles."

"Doubling the shake shingles won't be a problem since they haven't shipped yet," Bob said. "But if we return half of this load, you're going to have to pay a handling fee plus the standard mileage rate for us to return it to the yard. Those are the terms of your contract."

Arden didn't know what to do. He and Ivan had budgeted down to the penny for inventory. They couldn't afford to pay for a surplus like this right now. But it would be a complete waste of money to pay for the drivers to return the wood to the lumberyard.

"All right. We'll keep it."

When they finished unloading and stacking as much of the lumber as they could on the racks that weren't already filled with pine, they piled the rest of it on the floor.

"Per your contract, there's a 10 percent discount if you pay us now," Bob told him.

Arden wished he would have read the contract or that Bob had reminded him of the discount while they were unloading—it would have given him more time to write the check. Arden wrote especially slowly if he felt as if someone was breathing down his neck. His pen hovered over the payee line.

"How do you spell *Knight's* again?" he asked, and the taller guy snickered while Bob dictated the spelling.

As they sauntered away, Arden heard the wiry man remark to Bob, "I guess someone who graduated from a one-room schoolhouse isn't going to win any spelling bees, huh?"

"Maybe not, but he sure does nice work," Bob replied, gesturing toward the playhouse. "Wish I could afford something like that for my kid. It's nicer than my *own* home."

Arden's face was still hot when his sister walked through the door some ten minutes later. "What's wrong, Grace? Is *Mamm* okay?"

"*Jah*, she's fine. Rebecca Miller is visiting her, so I came over with cheeseburger *supp* to put in Ivan's freezer, along with *kuche* for his pantry. I know other women in the district will be bringing him meals when he's discharged from the hospital, but I want him to have plenty to choose from while he's recovering."

"Oh. I, um, don't know if that's a *gut* idea."

"Why not? Doesn't he like cheeseburger *supp*?"

"*Neh*, that's not it." Arden knew Ivan hadn't wanted anyone to find out about Rachel coming, lest Colin interfered and stopped her. Now that Rachel had arrived, Arden figured it was only a matter of time until Colin and his family learned of her presence—and even when they did, there was little they could do about it. Still, he was reluctant to be the one to spill the beans. "His, uh, *schweschder* is visiting. She's staying in his *haus.*"

"His sister? The *schmaert* one who became an *Englisch* nurse?"

Arden bristled at the mention of Rachel's intelligence. "Ivan only has *one* sister. And *jah*, Rachel's a nurse."

"She's *kumme* to take care of him?"

While Arden would have preferred it if other people believed Rachel had come specifically to take care of Ivan rather than to help Arden with business matters, that wouldn't explain why she'd arrived when Ivan was still in the hospital. "*Jah*, and to, uh, help with some of the administrative tasks at the shop—since I'll be too busy making sheds to do the paperwork."

"That's *wunderbaar.* Since she's a nurse, maybe she'll take a look at the skin on *Mamm*'s fingers. Is Rachel at the *haus* now? I could go introduce—"

"*Neh!*" It was going to be challenging enough to work with Rachel every day; Arden didn't want her flaunting her smarts in his home, too. Nor did he want his mother trying to pair them up; she'd been nagging him for nearly two years to go to a matchmaker in a neighboring district in Unity. She claimed she couldn't go home to heaven in good conscience until both of her children found spouses. Arden invariably replied if that was the case, he had a responsibility to remain single indefinitely. It had become a running joke between them, but Arden sensed his mother was more serious than she let on. Knowing her, it wouldn't matter that Rachel was no longer Amish—she'd insist Rachel could be wooed back into the fold. Arden, however, was not in a wooing state of mind.

"Rachel's not home. If *Mamm* needs medical care, we'll take her to the *dokder*. I don't want you to ask Rachel for help. For all intents and purposes, she's an *Englischer*. We can work with her, and of course we'll be kind to her, but that doesn't mean she's invited to our *haus* to socialize. Besides, she probably prefers her privacy. In any case, Ivan asked me to keep the news of her arrival to myself, so I trust you'll do the same."

His sister narrowed her eyes, but she didn't argue. "Okay, but I'm going to go put the *supp* in Ivan's fridge so Rachel can enjoy something *gut* to eat when she comes home, just like you do every evening, Arden. Except *she'll* have to eat hers alone."

Her point made, Grace tugged the door shut behind her. The force caused the mail to slide from Ivan's desk for the umpteenth time, as if to emphasize just how much Arden needed Rachel's help.

Rachel spoke with a nurse before entering Ivan's room, confirming what she already imagined; for a few days, Ivan's health had been hanging in the balance. He'd had a severe case of bacterial pneumonia and then suffered a reaction to the antibiotics, rendering it difficult for the doctors to determine the most effective course of treatment. He was still on oxygen and needed to remain in the hospital for several more days, but yesterday there had been indications his condition was finally improving.

After not seeing him for ten years, the sight of her

brother would have moved Rachel deeply even if he hadn't been lying in a hospital bed, but his pale, manly face and thin, limp body overwhelmed her, despite her professional training. She spent the better part of the afternoon sitting beside him, stroking his dark wispy hair or resting her hand on his arm, praying. Whenever a nurse entered, she'd inquire about Ivan's medication and symptoms. Although plenty of patients in various stages of pneumonia visited the clinic, she'd never actively cared for them in an ongoing capacity, and she wanted to know what to watch for once Ivan returned home.

Some time around five o'clock, she must have dozed off, because she was awoken by a slight fluttering beneath her hand. Ivan was reaching to remove his oxygen mask.

"Neh," she said, slipping into *Deitsch.* "Don't try to talk, Ivan. Just let me look at you."

Now that he'd opened his big brown eyes, Rachel spotted a trace of the fourteen-year-old boy—her little brother—he'd been the last time she saw him, and she smiled as she bent forward to give him a hug. "I'm sorry you've been so sick. I came as soon as I heard."

She felt him nodding against her cheek, and she held him a moment longer before letting go. She pulled her chair closer and peered into his eyes. "I don't want you to worry about anything at the shop. I'll stay as long as you need. You just focus on resting and getting better."

He nodded and reached for the mask once more. Pulling it up, he asked in a whisper, "Have you seen…" That was all he could manage, so she had to guess what he meant.

"The workshop? It looks great. So large and professional. You've clearly done well."

But he shook his head so she guessed again.

"I've met Arden, *jah.*" But Ivan closed his eyes to indicate that wasn't his question, either. "Have I seen Colin and his family?"

Ivan nodded, wincing. It occurred to Rachel he was worried. But was he worried for her or for Colin and his family? Probably both. Ivan had been put in a difficult position when she left Serenity Ridge; he was so fond of Rachel and yet he was still under Colin and Hadassah's thumbs. By the time he was an adult and Colin and Hadassah had moved into their own house, Ivan had probably had enough of a challenge convincing his brothers he could start a business without creating more trouble by inviting Rachel home or traveling to visit her.

"I haven't seen them yet, *neh.* But don't worry, I'll do my best not to say anything to upset them. I won't let anything they say upset me, either." *It's not as if they can upset me more than they have by refusing to have any contact with me for the past ten years.* "We all just want you to get better."

Ivan nodded, his eyelids drooping. Now that she'd seen him, Rachel was reluctant to let her brother out of her sight again, but he'd rest more soundly without her there. She gave him another hug. "I'm going to go, but I'll visit again tomorrow afternoon. I'll call the nursing station and check in on you in the morning, and they can call me any time you want them to, as well."

She thought he'd already fallen asleep, but as Rachel turned to leave, Ivan's fingertips brushed her sleeve. She paused as he lifted his mask a third time. "*Denki,* Ray-Ray," he said. It was what he'd called her when he was learning to talk, and the nickname made Rachel smile and tear up at the same time.

I haven't cried so much in one day since...since the day I left Serenity Ridge, she thought.

On the way home, she stopped at a superstore to purchase a cell phone charger and some groceries. She was so weary she grabbed a couple of microwave entrees and didn't realize her mistake until she was driving out of the parking lot, but she was too tired to turn around. Maybe she could pry the frozen food out of its plastic containers and heat it in the gas oven.

Arden's been caring for the animals. I wonder what he's done with the eggs he's collected... Rachel didn't realize how fortunate she'd been to grow up with an endless supply of fresh eggs until she moved to Boston. On Saturdays she'd drive fifteen miles to the farmer's market to buy them, although they were outrageously expensive. As far as she was concerned, she'd be happy to eat fresh eggs morning, noon and night for the duration of her stay in Serenity Ridge.

Then she wondered if Arden would still be working. No, it was close to seven o'clock, and he would have gone home for supper by now. Ivan never wrote about Arden's family, but since Arden didn't have a beard, Rachel deduced he wasn't married, which didn't exactly surprise her. While Arden was undeniably handsome, the Amish valued good character over good looks, and Rachel didn't know quite what to make of his personality. Not only was he uncommunicative, but he seemed humorless, too. Still, he'd appeared sincerely apologetic about having given her such a scare, and Ivan thought highly of him, so he had to have redeeming qualities, even if Rachel didn't know what they were yet.

There was no buggy or horse in the yard when she arrived home, although she hadn't remembered seeing one the first time she'd arrived, either. Maybe Arden lived close enough to walk? Suddenly Rachel felt uneasy staying alone in the big house, without any neighbors within shouting distance. She had to remind herself she wasn't in the city anymore. She was safer here, but she intended to lock the door anyway.

When she set down the groceries, she discovered a note on the kitchen table.

Welcome, Rachel—
I thought you'd enjoy soup—it's in the fridge, and I've filled the cookie jar with snickerdoodles.
    I hope to meet you soon.
Grace Esh (Arden's sister)

Why such a sweet note and an even sweeter act of kindness should reduce Rachel to tears—*again*—she didn't know, but they did. And few things made Rachel as ravenous as crying, so after a day of bawling her eyes out, she tossed the frozen dinners into the freezer of the gas-powered refrigerator and heated the soup instead. When she finished eating a large bowl of it, she still felt hungry, so she had a second bowl, followed by two cookies.

Finally, too full and exhausted to think another thought, Rachel collapsed into bed.

On Saturday morning, Arden was relieved to find the cow had been milked and the eggs collected at Ivan's place. He'd been caring for the animals and bringing the surplus dairy products home so the deacon's wife could share them with those in need. Ivan was glad to relinquish the responsibility, but it surprised him a city girl had gotten up so early on a Saturday.

When he came out of the barn, he was further surprised to see Rachel crossing the lawn carrying two cups of coffee. Tinted red by the morning sun, her hair was an eye-catching contrast with her creamy complexion. For an *Englischer*, she didn't seem to wear much makeup. *Not that she needs any, but I wonder if she's going without it so she'll fit in with the Amish women in Serenity Ridge?* Arden quickly dismissed the curious thought. *"Guder mariye."*

"Guder mariye."

It wasn't until Rachel replied in kind that Arden realized he'd greeted her in *Deitsch*. She didn't seem to bat an eye, but he wondered if he ought to address her solely in *Englisch* instead. She extended a mug to him. He'd already had coffee before leaving his house, but he never refused another cup. He accepted it and held the workshop door open for her.

"Ivan must have told you we usually work from seven or eight o'clock until noon on Saturday. But I didn't think you'd be up and at 'em at this hour."

Rachel's response was peppered with even more *Deitsch* words. "I get up earlier than this to commute to work. Besides, I couldn't wait to have fresh *oier* for breakfast. They were *appenditlich*. So were the *kuche* and *supp* your *schweschder* made."

"My *schweschder*?" Ivan wondered how Rachel knew it was his sister who'd left the goodies in her kitchen.

"*Jah.* That's how she identified herself in her note. Grace Esh. She *is* your *schweschder*, isn't she?" Rachel tittered, and Arden gritted his teeth. By saying such stupid things in front of her, he kept opening himself up to her teasing. Or was it mockery?

He motioned toward the desk, ignoring her question. "You might want to get started on the paperwork by going through that stack of mail. Our calendar is somewhere beneath all those papers, and it'll show you what we've got scheduled when. The checkbook's in the bottom drawer. We had a delivery from Knight's yesterday and got a 10 percent discount. I wrote out a check, but I didn't record the amount in the ledger yet. Also, Mrs. McGregor wants the playhouse completed a week early, so please call our delivery guy and arrange for that."

"Whoa! Wait a second," Rachel protested, setting her mug on a large manila envelope. "How do you expect me to remember all of that? Let me grab a pen... Where *is* a pen?"

Before Arden could answer, the door swung open, and Colin Blank walked in. Rachel was crouched behind the desk, searching the drawer for a writing utensil, and she didn't immediately see him, so Arden announced loudly, "*Guder mariye*, Colin," which caused Rachel to jump up.

"*Guder mariye*, Arden." Then, catching sight of his sister, he said stiffly in *Englisch*, "Hello, Rachel."

"*Guder mariye*, Colin. It's—it's *gut* to see you," Rachel replied. Arden noticed her hands were trembling as she lifted her arms, presumably to embrace her brother, who remained motionless. Rachel quickly dropped her arms, knocking her hand against the desk and jostling her cup, which sloshed coffee onto the mail.

As Rachel used a blank sheet of paper to blot the

spill, Arden took advantage of the pause to edge away, saying, "I'll, uh, let the two of you talk in private."

"*Neh*, don't leave. What I've *kumme* to say concerns you both." Colin announced, "Last evening Hadassah and I visited Ivan in the hospital. Imagine our surprise when the nurse told us Rachel had been there to see him, too. And that she'll be helping care for him after he's discharged."

Uh-oh. Arden had known this moment of familial reckoning would come, but he hadn't expected to be in the middle of it. Neither he nor Rachel spoke—Colin had a commanding presence.

"Even more perplexing was that Ivan indicated Rachel will be helping with the paperwork here," Colin said. Arden noticed he avoided addressing his sister directly; instead, he referred to her in the third person, as if she weren't standing a few feet away. "Since he couldn't elaborate, we figured we must have misunderstood him. Would you care to explain?"

Arden swallowed, unsure if Colin was speaking to him or to Rachel. "I-I-I'll be too b-busy constructing the sheds to take care of our orders and accounting."

"I understand what it's like to be short-staffed," Colin said. "What I'm confused about is why you didn't ask me or Hadassah or someone from our district for assistance."

Arden tried to think of a diplomatic yet truthful explanation. He couldn't well say, *You're so reproachful Ivan was worried you'd find fault with our business and try to convince us to close shop.* Nor could Arden admit he didn't want others in their district to discover the extent of his reading and writing difficulty. Fortunately, Rachel piped up.

"From what I understand, many in the community are preparing for planting season, and spring is an extremely busy time for you at work, too, especially with Albert being in Canada. And Hadassah's pregnancy is wearing her out, so Ivan didn't want to burden the two of you."

Colin's face visibly reddened, and Arden didn't know if it was because the Amish in their district avoided using the word *pregnancy*, especially in mixed company, or if he was angry because Rachel had answered instead of Arden, but there was no mistaking his insinuation when he said, "Ivan, Hadassah and I are *familye*, and *familye* help carry each other's burdens."

Rachel lifted her chin, clearly unfazed. "*Jah*, which is exactly why *I'm* here—to help my *bruder* Ivan, as well as my *bruder* in Christ, Arden."

Upon being reminded of their shared Christian faith, Colin appeared to momentarily back down. His posture softened. "It was kind of you to *kumme*, Rachel, but I'll help Arden with the accounting and orders, and Hadassah and the other women in our district will care for Ivan when he comes home from the hospital. I'm sorry for the inconvenience of traveling all this way, but there's no need for you to stay any longer."

"*Denki* for your concern about me, Colin." Rachel's response was equally tempered. "But it's a privilege, not an inconvenience, for me to be here. I gave Ivan my word I'd stay and help, and I intend to honor my promise."

Colin acted as if she hadn't spoken. Directing his gaze toward Arden, he said, "Ivan is ill, so I understand his lapse in judgment, but I would have thought you'd know better. You should have asked me for help."

Arden resented Colin scolding him as if he were a child, but not as much as he resented it when Rachel called attention to Colin scolding him as if he were a child. "Arden's not a *bu* and you're not his *daed.* You wouldn't appreciate it if someone came into *your* shop and took over *your* business," she pointed out.

Now the brother and sister were speaking as if *Arden* weren't there, and it riled him to no end, but even if he had known what to say, they didn't give him an opportunity to say it.

"Your opinion is not *wilkom,* so I'd thank you not to interfere," Colin authoritatively declared. "This matter is between Arden and me."

"*Neh,* this matter is between Ivan and Arden. *You're* the one who's interfering."

Colin must have been surprised by the fire in Rachel's voice, or else he recognized he was overstepping, because he faltered. "All—all right, then. Arden, do you want Rachel or me to help you with the administration of the shop?"

Some decisions were easier than others. "Rachel," Arden stated definitely.

Both Rachel's and Colin's mouths dropped open. Colin recovered first, saying, "If that is your decision, I'll respect it." He clapped Arden on the back. "But if you change your mind or if there's anything else I can do to support you, let me know."

Once the door closed behind Colin, Rachel clasped her hands beneath her chin and gushed, "*Denki* for standing up for me like that. It means a lot to me."

Considering how poorly Colin had treated Rachel, Arden could understand why she'd feel like Arden had stood up for her, but he didn't want her getting the wrong idea. "I wasn't standing up for you. I was abiding by an agreement I made with my business partner," he told her. "If Ivan had suggested we ask Colin for help, I would have agreed to honor that request, too."

"*Jah*, I know. I just meant...never mind." Pressing her lips together, Rachel turned her back toward him and began tearing open an envelope.

If her presence is going to cause me this much stress every day, I might need to convince Ivan to take Colin up on his offer to help, Arden thought to himself as he strode to the opposite end of the workshop, where he could labor in peace.

Chapter Three

On Sunday morning as Rachel drove into town to attend a local church, she passed the little building the Amish used for worship. Although most Amish throughout the country took turns hosting biweekly services in their homes, the Serenity Ridge and Unity districts were two of a few exceptions that worshipped in church buildings. However, they did keep the custom of only gathering every other week as a congregation; on alternating Sundays, families met in their own homes. Rachel was surprised to see the number of buggies neatly lined along the perimeter of the property; could the community have grown that much since she'd been away, or did a lot of folks have relatives visiting?

She sighed. The Amish practice of visiting each other on Sunday afternoons had been one of her favorite customs when she was young. As a girl outnumbered by three brothers, Rachel relished any opportunity that allowed her to socialize with female friends. Once she became a teenager, she better appreciated having older brothers whose male friends dropped in at their house. Although Colin and Albert's friends were too old to have any romantic interest in Rachel, that didn't stop her from developing crushes on them. By the time she was mature enough to have a suitor, she'd already made up her mind to leave the Amish, which was probably just as well, considering there weren't any eligible bachelors her age in their tiny district anyway.

Maybe there are more courting opportunities now that the community has grown, she thought. Ivan hadn't ever written about walking out with anyone, but she wouldn't have expected him to, since the Amish were more discreet about their romantic relationships than the *Englisch* were. Still, she couldn't help but wonder if he was courting anyone. Then she found herself wondering whether Arden was courting anyone, and if so, whether they'd be walking out tonight, the way Amish couples often did on Sunday evenings. *Why would I care?* she asked herself. *It's certainly not as if I want him to pay* me *a visit instead.*

But as she headed home after church, Rachel had to admit she wished *someone* would drop by; the house seemed too large and lonely. *Maybe I should make the first move and visit Colin, Hadassah and the children,* she thought. *I could offer to take them to see Ivan.* Ultimately, she wasn't that brave, however, so she journeyed to the hospital alone, where her brother slept through most of her visit.

A downpour broke out as Rachel drove home, and when she trekked across the lawn, her shoes left a trail of indented footprints behind her. "Mud season" was what Mainers called the period in between late March and early May when the ground was oversaturated with melted winter snow and fresh spring rain. Rachel recalled how she and Hadassah sometimes had to mop the floors three times a day to keep up with the muck her brothers tracked in.

Being back in Serenity Ridge was stirring all kinds of memories, some happier than others. Rachel remembered sledding with her brothers in the winter and the long afternoons her mother had spent teaching her to bake and sew. She even recalled how excited she'd been to help plan for Colin's wedding to Hadassah—and how that excitement turned to disappointment when Hadassah moved into their house and Rachel found out how controlling she was. Then there were her parents' funerals, as well as her own leaving...

Aware her mood would darken if she thought too much about the past, Rachel took out the ingredients she'd purchased on Saturday and set about making a batch of sticky buns the way her mother had taught her. Because the recipe made far more buns than she could eat by herself, she decided to bring a half dozen of them to the workshop the next morning, along with coffee for Arden and her. They'd gotten off on the wrong foot, but as her mother always told her, there was nothing like fresh confections and friendly conversation to draw people together. Granted, Arden had made a point of letting her know it made no difference to him whether he worked with her or with Colin, as long as Ivan's preference was honored, but Rachel figured since she *was* the one working there, she'd try to foster a cordial environment. She was tickled when her efforts seemed to pay off.

"These are really *gut*," Arden said, his mouth half-full.

"*Denki*. I was worried I may have lost my touch. It's been ages since I've made them."

"Why? Don't you like them?"

"I *love* them." Rachel pulled a bun off the loaf for herself. "I got out of practice because, well, my ex-boyfriend, Toby, used to lecture me about the detrimental effects of sugar."

"Is he diabetic?"

"No. He's a *dokder*. And he's right—an excess of sugar *can* be bad for you."

"An excess of *anything* can be bad for you." Arden took a swallow of coffee before adding, "I'm surprised you'd let his opinion stop you from doing something you wanted to do."

Despite her intentions to establish a congenial relationship, Rachel was immediately defensive. "Just because I left the Amish against my family's wishes doesn't mean—"

"I wasn't referring to your leaving the Amish," Arden interrupted. "I was referring to your refusal to back down to Colin's demands the other day. *I* even had a difficult time saying no to him, but you held your own. So it surprises me you'd give in to your boyfriend's opinion about sticky buns. Seems to me, if he didn't want to eat them, he didn't have to, but why should that stop you from making them if that's what you enjoy doing?"

Rachel shrugged, dumbfounded. For all the times people had implied she was strong-willed, it had never come across as a compliment until now, and she treasured Arden's words. At the same time, she felt criticized by his remark about her deference to Toby... Was that because Arden was right? "I guess I sort of figured he...well, he's a *dokder* and he knows a lot more about health than I do."

Brushing the crumbs from his lips with the back of

his hand, Arden remarked, "*Jah*, he knows a lot more about health than I do, too, but that doesn't mean I'm not going to have a second sticky bun after lunch today."

As she watched him effortlessly pick up a drill and ladder and carry them across the workshop, Rachel's heart skipped two beats in a row. *It's probably from all the sugar I just ate*, she tried to convince herself.

Arden leaned the ladder against the double wood storage shed and climbed a few steps to inspect the roof a final time before it was picked up for delivery the following day. Made from rough-cut lumber, the structure required no painting, which was a relief, since painting was the task Arden favored the least. As it was, he was dreading painting the inside of the playhouse. Although the cost of any building they constructed included a painted exterior, Ivan and Arden agreed it wasn't worth it to them in terms of time to paint the interiors, so they left that chore to the customers. Mrs. McGregor, however, had insisted she'd pay extra if they'd accommodate her request this one time. It was important to her that the playhouse be delivered in "move-in–ready condition," as she put it, which was also why she'd supplied her daughter's favorite hue of paint.

It's strange, the things Englischers *will indulge in*, he thought. *And even stranger what they won't.* He could understand why too many sweets could be bad for a person—it didn't take a medical degree to realize how important a healthy diet was—but he took Rachel's ex-boyfriend's opinion about sticky buns as a criticism of the Amish lifestyle. *It's probable some of us eat more sweets than* Englischers*, but our desserts aren't loaded with preservatives. Not to mention, we get a lot more* *exercise than the average* Englischer, *and we've been eating farm-to-table food since long before they came up with the term.*

Arden hopped down from the ladder and glanced across the room at Rachel, who was holding a paper in one hand and running her finger down another paper that lay flat on the desk. She appeared to be cross-referencing documents. Arden hoped she could figure out her brother's abbreviations, notes and figures, because Arden sure wouldn't be able to offer any input—a fact he didn't want her to discover. *Someone who dates a doctor would find it hard to fathom how a grown man can't comprehend simple record-keeping.*

Rachel happened to look up and caught him watching her. Giving a little smile, she asked, "Is there something you need from me?"

"I—I wanted to be sure the pickup is scheduled for this shed for tomorrow."

She set down the paper she was holding and opened the planner; like Ivan, she was very organized and had already decluttered the desk. After surveying it, she rose and brought the planner to him. Pointing at a line half-way down the page, she said, "I think this *PU* means pickup, right? But what's *RCWS*? The customer's initials?"

Arden chewed the inside of his cheek. He would have been hard-pressed to answer even if Rachel hadn't been standing so close to him, but he was especially distracted by the little scar above her right cheekbone. It reminded him of a tiny chip in a delicate teacup. "I, uh, I think the cu-customer's last name is Johnston. There should be a customer folder in the filing cabinet."

"I'll check on the name and address, but that still

won't tell me if the pickup has been scheduled. To be safe, I'd better call the trucking company," she decided. Motioning to the shed, she remarked, "It's beautiful. I love the look of natural wood. What do you call wood like that?"

"The wood is cedar, but the way it is sawn is called rough cut. I like rough-cut sheds best myself, too."

"That's it!" Rachel grabbed his forearm. "*RCWS* means rough-cut wood shed."

It was either her hand on his arm or sheer embarrassment about his ignorance that was making Arden feel overly warm. He pulled away and reached to retract the ladder so she couldn't see his face. "*Jah*, that makes sense. Sorry, I must have forgotten."

"Don't apologize—it's a crazy recording system. I'm just *hallich* we cracked the code."

Relieved Rachel didn't think he was a dolt for not knowing the acronym, Arden confessed, "To be honest, Ivan takes care of most of the paperwork around here, so your guess is as *gut* as mine when it comes to figuring it out—actually, your guess is *better* than mine."

"If that's true, it's because I'm related to him. Our minds must be wired the same way." Rachel's eyes twinkled with more green than brown today. "Which probably explains why we were so close as *kinner.*"

"Seems like you're still pretty close, otherwise he wouldn't have asked for your help," Arden acknowledged, which seemed to brighten Rachel's expression even more.

"Do you have other *brieder* or *schweschdere*?"

"*Neh*, just Grace," he answered. "She lives with me, along with my *mamm*. I moved here from Indiana when I heard about the opportunity to work with Ivan. Then

I brought my *mamm* and Grace out after my *daed* died a few years ago."

"Do you miss your community in Indiana?"

"*Jah*, but this is my community now. It's where my *familye* and my *kurrich familye* live, so it's home to me."

A shadow crossed Rachel's face, and Arden realized he might have sounded as if he were judging her for leaving the Amish, which he wasn't. That's what happened when he volunteered too much information—he said the wrong things even if he managed to use the right words.

"That reminds me, I'm going to visit Hadassah during my lunch break today," Rachel said. "I'll take the business phone with me, in case a customer calls."

"Are you sure you want to do that?" Arden asked. He meant was she sure she wanted to take the business phone, but she must have thought he was asking if she was sure she wanted to visit Hadassah.

"*Jah*. I'm going to offer her and Colin a ride to the hospital whenever they want to visit Ivan," she answered. "And that offer is open to anyone in the community, including you."

Given how quickly rumors spread in Serenity Ridge, Arden couldn't imagine traveling alone with *any* woman, much less with a woman who'd "gone *Englisch*." Still, he thanked her for her thoughtful offer, and they resumed working until their one o'clock lunch break.

"I left your sugar fix wrapped up in the bottom drawer," Rachel said with a sassy grin before she exited the workshop.

"My sugar fix?"

"*Jah*, the sticky buns, remember? I'm not going to

eat any more of those since I have plenty at the *haus*, so help yourself. There's four left."

"Only four?" he joked back. "The Amish require six servings of fresh goodies a day."

"*Ach*, I forgot," she said, pretending to smack her forehead. "I'll bring more tomorrow."

It made Arden inexplicably happy that he could still hear her laughing even after she'd closed the door behind her.

Rachel hesitated in the driveway, wondering whether she should drive or take the buggy. She didn't want to offend Hadassah by showing up in a car, but she didn't have a lot of time to spare, so she went inside to fetch her keys. Passing a mirror, she realized she should do something to her hair, which hung loosely about her face and shoulders. It would have been hypocritical to pull it back in a bun the way the Amish women did, but out of respect to her sister-in-law, she brushed it into a ponytail. She was already wearing a long navy blue skirt, and while her cotton top was short-sleeved—most Amish women in Serenity Ridge wore sleeves that covered their elbows—it was plain white and had a modest neckline.

Although she'd felt encouraged her attempt to break the ice with Arden had been so successful, when Rachel pulled into the driveway leading to Colin and Hadassah's home, she lost her confidence. She didn't expect to be *welcomed*, but what if her sister-in-law wouldn't even *acknowledge* her? There was only one way to find out. As she followed the path to the house, Rachel carefully avoided the puddles leftover from yesterday's rain. Muddy shoes would give Hadassah an extra reason not to invite her in, and Rachel really wanted to meet her nieces and nephews who hadn't yet been born by the time she left.

Colin and Hadassah had gotten married when Rachel was fifteen, and by the time she left home, they had one daughter, with a baby boy on the way. Two years later, Ivan wrote that Rachel's sister-in-law had had another girl, and three years after that, another boy. Sadly, she'd lost a baby, too—Rachel had sent a letter of condolence, which, like the other letters, went unanswered. Although it would be considered too bold to inquire, she hoped Hadassah's current pregnancy was progressing smoothly and the unborn twins were healthy.

Rachel's legs felt weak as she reached the front porch, where a boy about five years old was sitting on the steps. "Hello," she greeted him. "I'm your *ant*. You must be Thomas."

The boy furrowed his brows. "My *ant* went to Canada with *Onkel* Albert."

"*Jah*, that's your *ant* Joyce. I'm your *ant* Rachel."

"I don't have an *ant* Rachel," the boy contradicted. He wasn't being rude—Rachel doubted Colin or Hadassah had told him about her. It stung, but she couldn't blame his parents. They would have feared they'd negatively influence their children by merely presenting the possibility someone could leave the Amish.

"Would you please tell your *mamm* that Rachel is here to see her?"

Hadassah appeared at the screen door. "Thomas, your lunch is on the table. Take your boots off by the entrance and go join your *bruder* and *schweschdere*." She held open the door and turned to the side so he could pass.

Squinting up at her from the bottom step, Rachel noticed Hadassah's belly was so large she appeared to be nearing the end of her pregnancy, although with twins, it was sometimes difficult to tell. "Hello, Hadassah." Her voice quavered as she fought to control her emotions. Her sister-in-law had always had a way of making Rachel feel she was intruding, even when Hadassah came to live in *Rachel's* house.

She remained on the other side of the door. "What can I do for you, Rachel?"

Her manner told Rachel what she'd already suspected; she was going to be treated like an outsider, or at best, like a customer. *You could invite me in and introduce me to my nieces and nephews.* "I wanted to say hello and ask if you need a ride to the hospital. I'm *hallich* to—"

"*Neh*, we don't want to ride in an *automobile*. We'll get there on our own."

"But it's too far away to take the horse," Rachel began to say. Then she realized it wasn't that Hadassah didn't want to ride in a car—it was that she didn't want to ride in *Rachel's* car. She swallowed, trying not to feel slighted. "Okay, well, if you change your mind, let me know. And once Ivan is discharged, please feel free to stop by the house any time."

"*Denki*—I mean thank you," Hadassah said as if Rachel no longer understood *Deitsch*. "It's good to know you're allowing Ivan's relatives to visit him. His brothers will be so pleased."

There, that did it; Rachel's eyes welled with tears. "I didn't mean I was *allowing* you. I meant I'd *wilkom* your company." *Even though you're being terrible to me.*

The silence that followed was punctuated by birdsong and the muffled conversation of the children inside. If Rachel heard correctly, her name was mentioned. She waited another moment before saying, "I'd better get back now. I've been helping Arden with the bookkeeping, and I'm having a hard time making heads or tails of Ivan's notes," she nervously admitted.

"Colin could take over if you're struggling," Hadassah suggested.

Rachel's cheeks burned. Hadassah was just *looking* for a reason to get rid of her. "*Denki*, but I'll figure it out. Besides, it keeps me busy until Ivan is discharged."

"If you're bored, you should consider returning to your job in the city. Joyce will be back from Ontario soon. Between the two of us and the deacon's wife, Jaala, we can care for Ivan. We might not have nursing degrees, but we'll see to it he recovers."

Rachel refused to respond in kind to Hadassah's barbed insinuations. As genuinely as she could, she replied, "*Denki*, but I'd rather stay here until Ivan is better. I'd *wilkom* your help caring for him, though. And if you change your mind about a ride, let me know..."

Rachel forgot she'd been standing on the first stair and she stumbled as she backed away, narrowly missing a puddle, but she didn't stop moving until she reached the end of the road, where she pulled over and put the car in Park. Resting her head upon her arms on the steering wheel, she tried to gather her swirling thoughts. *Why does Hadassah tear me down like that?* I'm *not the one who acts as if I'm better than she is—she's got so much* hochmut *she'd rather pay exorbitant cab fare than accept a ride from me! And I never implied she couldn't effectively help Ivan recover—even if I* do *know more about health care than she does.*

The abrupt honking of a loud horn caused Rachel to lift her head and peek in the rearview mirror. She rolled down her window and motioned for the driver to go around her; there was plenty of room. *You might as well pass me,* she thought belligerently, *because I'm not leaving until I'm good and ready to leave.* And that warning went double for her sister-in-law.

Arden sighed as he put away his insulated lunch bag. Having completed the shed for pickup, he could move on to the next one. He also had a doghouse to build. Arden and Ivan frequently joked the business should be named Blank's Little Buildings instead of Blank's Sheds, because they accepted orders for everything from sheds to ice shanties to doghouses. They'd even built an outhouse once. As long as a building's dimensions fell within the state's regulations for transportation, they could make it, but Arden was looking forward to the day when they could focus solely on sheds, because they could be more efficient that way. But until their business grew, they couldn't turn away any projects, including playhouses. Which meant this afternoon Arden had to tackle the task he least enjoyed: painting.

He'd just finished rolling paint over the first wall when someone entered the workshop. Unable to tell whether it was Rachel or a customer, he squeezed through the playhouse door. It was Rachel. Her face was blotchy and her eyes pink-rimmed, like on the day he met her. Uh-oh. Her visit with her sister-in-law must not have gone well.

Arden could sympathize; Colin's behavior toward her the other day had been downright spiteful. You'd think under the circumstances, he'd extend Rachel a little grace. After all, Ivan had been gravely ill and Rachel was volunteering in the shop. Arden supposed it was none of his business how the Blanks interacted, but it wouldn't hurt if he showed a little more appreciation of Rachel himself.

"Hi," he said casually, strolling in her direction to grab a rag from the bin.

"Hi." She barely glanced up from the planner she had already opened in front of her. "If I'm reading this right, it looks like there's another shed that's due on Monday."

"*Jah.* I'll get right on that as soon as I finish painting the inside of the playhouse."

This time she paused to look up. One side of her mouth lifted in a wry smile. "Lavender?"

"How did you know?"

Rachel pointed to her own hair, which he noticed she'd pulled into a ponytail, to indicate he had something on *his* head. "The flecks gave you away."

Arden scowled, pulling a curl straight and checking his fingers for paint. "It's *lecherich*, the things the *Englisch* want."

Now Rachel scowled, too. "*Jah*, we're a *lecherich* group, aren't we?"

"*Neh*, I wasn't referring to *you*."

"I'm *Englisch* now."

Arden was trying to cheer her up, not offend her. He would have been better off if he'd remained inside the purple playhouse. "*Jah*, but—but—"

She waved her hand. "It's okay, I agree. Some *Englischers* buy their *kinner* too much stuff they don't need. I mean, considering the homelessness problem in our country, it seems extravagant for someone to buy a *kind* a playhouse she'll outgrow in a year or two.

But at least if they're going to buy something like that, it's *schmaert* they're investing in a playhouse as nice as the one you made."

"Denki," Arden said as warmth traveled from his ears all the way down his spine. "I hope the customer still thinks it's nice when it's delivered on Friday and she sees my paint job. I'm not the best painter, and it's close quarters in there."

Rachel snapped her fingers. "Oh no, I forgot to reschedule the pickup for that. Listen, how about if I make the call and then I'll do the painting so you can start on the next shed?"

Arden was taken aback. "That's very kind, but you don't have to do that. It's enough that you're managing the paperwork—"

"Really," she insisted, looking directly at him. Maybe it was because her hair was drawn up or because she'd been crying, but she appeared pallid, almost gaunt. "There's not enough paperwork for me to do while I'm waiting for a customer to call. Besides, I find the monotony of painting soothing. Especially when I'm using a soft color, like lavender."

"Lavender paint has the opposite effect on me," Arden said with a laugh. "But even with its windows open, the playhouse doesn't have a lot of ventilation. I don't want you to get dizzy."

"I carry surgical masks wherever I go. I'll grab one from my car."

So, while Arden went to work on the next shed, Rachel painted the playhouse interior. Every once in a while he'd call out, asking how she was doing in there, and she'd indicate in a muffled voice she was fine.

Toward the end of the afternoon, she stuck her head

out and pulled off the mask. "*Kumme* take a look. Tell me if you see any spots I've missed."

Arden gingerly ducked into the playhouse—Mrs. McGregor had insisted he shouldn't add an adult-size door to the back of the structure because she wanted the house to be "child-centric"—and straightened his posture to three-quarters of his height. Rachel was as meticulous with her painting as Ivan was about his work. "I hate to admit it, but it looks really *gut.*"

"Hate to admit it? Why? Because *Englischers* can't paint as well as the Amish?"

"*Neh*, because it's purple."

Rachel blushed. "Sorry, I guess I'm a little defensive."

"A little?"

She chuckled. "I think it could use another coat, don't you?"

"It's hard to say until this coat dries."

"*Jah*, you're right. So what color do they want the trim painted?"

"I think she called it cloud white or cotton white—it was something fluffy." Arden instantly wished he hadn't admitted that was how he remembered the name of the paint—he sounded so juvenile.

"Poodle white, maybe?" Rachel joked, and from the way she rolled her eyes, he recognized she was poking fun at the names of the paint colors, not at him.

Suddenly, aware of how close they were to one another—not that there was any other way to position themselves in such a tight space—he felt heady and needed air. "I think the fumes are getting to me," he said. As he backed toward the door, he inadvertently stepped on the rim of the paint tray, upending it.

"Oh *neh*!" Rachel tried to scoop the spilled paint from the floor with her hands.

"Here, let me help," Arden offered, snatching the nearby rag. As he bent to swab the floor, she stood up, catching him beneath his chin, and he staggered backward. She reached for his arms to keep him from knocking into the wall, but it was too late; he could feel his shirt dampen with paint along his shoulders as well as on his arms where Rachel had clutched them.

"I am such a kl-l-lutz. I am so sorry. I ruined your wall."

"*I'm* sorry. I ruined your shirt. Look—your sleeves have handprints on them."

"Purple, my favorite color," Arden quipped as he gave Rachel the rag so she could wipe off her fingers. He twisted his torso to inspect his lower pant leg. A thick glob of paint dribbled down his calf to his ankle. "At least my shirt is color coordinated with my trousers."

That sent them into peals of laughter. Every time they tried to stop laughing, they'd start again, harder than before, until they were nearly breathless. Suddenly, Rachel went quiet. She held a lavender fingertip in the air in front of her lips. Arden listened. Someone had entered the workshop.

"Arden?" a man called.

Arden scrunched his shoulders forward so he wouldn't rub against the door frame as he exited the playhouse and Rachel followed. Colin was standing a few yards away, shaking his head. "What is going on here?"

"W-we—we," Arden stuttered, both embarrassed and angry. He could imagine how ridiculous he and

Rachel looked, but who was Colin to demand to know what was going on in *his* workshop?

"We spilled paint," Rachel said, an edge in her voice.

"That much is clear," Colin retorted. "Spilling paint is a waste of money—and time. It hardly seems like a laughing matter."

"I guess that depends on how good your sense of humor is," Rachel shot back. Sometimes it was difficult to say whether Colin was goading her or she was the one goading Colin, but Arden wished they'd both knock it off.

"Is—is Ivan okay?" he asked, concerned about the reason for Colin's visit.

"*Jah.* I spoke with the *dokder* this morning, and he said Ivan should be discharged by the end of the week. It would be a shame if he came back to find the workshop like this." He pointed at the hem of Arden's pants, which were dripping paint onto the floor.

So that Rachel wouldn't have a chance to interject a snippy reply, Arden quickly said, "Praise *Gott. Denki* for coming all this way to share the *gut* news with us, Colin."

"*Jah*, well..." Colin seemed thwarted by Arden's expression of gratitude. "I also brought you this estimate of Ivan's hospital bill. It's based on the premise he'll be in the hospital another four or five days. They won't tally the final amount until he's discharged, but I understand you and Ivan use your business earnings to cover medical bills. This will give you an idea of whether you can pay it or not."

The Amish oftentimes negotiated a steep discount with health-care providers by paying their bills in full at the time services were rendered. Ivan had always been more than generous in using their business profits to help cover Arden's mother's medical expenses, even forgoing his own salary on occasion. Now Ivan was the one who needed financial help. Arden had no doubt the community would cover whatever portion of Ivan's bill they could. But the collective funds were stretched to the limit, and he didn't want to strain them further. Arden knew roughly how much money he and Ivan had in their business account, and he could give up his salary for a couple of weeks, but with his mother sick, he couldn't be sure she wouldn't need to see a doctor again soon, too. Then what would happen? He didn't want Colin to find out they were financially strapped, lest he argue their situation was more evidence of why they should close their shop.

"Denki." Arden held out his hand for the estimate; his palm and fingertips were purple.

Colin shook his head. "I'll leave it on the desk so you can read it once you and Rachel are finished... spilling paint."

"What a grump," Rachel muttered as the door shut behind her brother. "So listen, I think the best thing is for you to take off your boots right there. Otherwise, you're going to leave purple prints everywhere you walk." She giggled, but Arden was no longer in a joking mood. She must have caught on, because she strode to the rag bin and returned with several more rags.

Blotting paint from his boots and pants, Arden realized Colin was right; he *had* wasted both money and time this afternoon, and he hoped Colin wouldn't tell Ivan about the paint incident. It wasn't so much that Arden cared about Colin's opinion as it was that Arden wanted Ivan to be confident Arden was doing everything that needed to be done in order to cover the hospital bill and meet their financial goals for the spring. And because the sooner Arden completed a project, the sooner he got paid, he was going to have to increase his productivity and decrease his distractions. *Which means keeping my conversations with Rachel to a minimum,* Arden decided. *Starting now.*

"I'm going to work late tonight, but after you've cleaned up the paint mess, you should leave for the evening," he told her when he finished wiping off his clothes.

"Are you sure? I could help—"

But Arden cut her off. "*Jah*, I'm sure," he said. *I'm absolutely positive.*

Chapter Four

Although Rachel visited Ivan on Monday and Tuesday, he'd been so groggy she'd barely begun to converse with him when he drifted off, so Wednesday evening she was thrilled to find him sitting up in bed, eating dinner—both good signs. Also, his oxygen face mask had been replaced with a nasal cannula, which made it easier for him to talk. "So, how are you and Arden getting along?" he asked in between spoonfuls of soup.

"He's kind of quiet, but we get along fine." In reality, except to thank Rachel for her help each day, Arden had hardly spoken two words to her since Colin's visit on Monday afternoon. The sudden switch in his attitude both offended Rachel and hurt her feelings, especially since they'd just broken the ice with each other, but there was no need to tell her brother that.

Ivan chuckled before responding, "*Neh*, I didn't mean how are you getting along with each other. I meant how are you getting along with the workload?"

"Oh!" Flustered, Rachel quickly recounted how, in between reconciling the business's accounts, fielding customer inquiries, stocking inventory and scheduling deliveries, she'd spent the past two days painting both the interior and exterior of the playhouse.

"You're really going above and beyond what we hoped you'd do for us. I appreciate it and I know Arden does, too, even though he's not much of a talker. It takes a while for him to open up, but once you get to know him, I think you'll find he's a *wunderbaar paerson*."

A wunderbaar paerson *wouldn't be influenced by such an* unfreindlich paerson *as our* bruder *Colin*, Rachel thought. Aloud, she paid Arden as much of an honest compliment as she could, admitting, "He does beautiful work on the sheds."

"*Jah*, I've learned a lot from watching him. I'm blessed to have him as my business partner and my *freind*," Ivan said, and it struck Rachel that as quick as Colin was to find fault with someone, Ivan was equally quick to compliment a person. She loved that quality in her younger brother, whether or not Arden deserved his praise. "Has he said anything about how his *mamm* has been feeling lately?"

"*Neh*. Why, what's wrong with his *mamm*?"

"She has lupus."

Rachel was surprised. Knowing Arden's mother had a chronic illness instantly made her feel less annoyed at him. As a nurse, Rachel frequently witnessed the toll a chronic illness could take on a patient's family members, as well as on the patient with the disease. "If she's having a flare, he didn't mention it."

"That figures. Arden tends to keep his struggles to himself. Have you met his *schweschder*, Grace?"

"*Neh*, although she left an *appenditlich* meal and dessert for me at the *haus*. I haven't met anyone from the community yet. I haven't seen anyone I used to know, either—except Colin and Hadassah." Until she said it aloud, Rachel didn't fully realize how much it bothered her that no one at all had dropped by Ivan's house to say hello.

"People from the community probably don't know you're here. I haven't been able to tell anyone because whenever I've gotten visitors, I've either been too sleepy or the oxygen mask has made it difficult for me to say much."

They know I'm here—everyone in Serenity Ridge always knows everything that's happening with everyone else, Rachel thought. *No one is stopping by because Colin and Hadassah have poisoned the well against me.* "It's all right, I don't mind being alone. Besides, pretty soon you'll be coming home, and you're the one I came to Serenity Ridge to see."

But for as independent as she thought she was, Rachel felt especially lonely that evening when she returned to the empty house. She called Meg, who launched into a story about how their upstairs neighbor had flooded the basement by cramming too much clothing into the washing machine. Meg didn't care about the puddles in the basement as much as she cared that the washer's agitator broke, so the machine was out of order and she had a mountain of laundry piling up. "What am I supposed to do now, wash everything by hand?"

"You mean like the Amish do?"

"The Amish wash their clothes by hand?"

"Sure. They beat them on rocks down at the river."

"They do?"

"No! Of course not, silly." Rachel giggled; some of the illusions *Englischers* held about the Amish amused her. Even though she'd educated her roommate on many

Amish practices, apparently she hadn't mentioned how the Amish in Serenity Ridge did their laundry. "They use old-fashioned wringer washers, which are powered by diesel generators. But they never use dryers—clothes are always hung on a line. I kind of miss doing that, because it makes everything smell fresh."

"I know exactly what you mean—my mother always hung out our laundry, too. It's funny, because these days people act so smug about buying energy-efficient dryers, but those same people wouldn't be caught dead hanging their clothes outside on a line."

Rachel laughed again. "Well, the Amish would consider using a dryer—even an energy-efficient one—to be as taboo as...as talking to *me*." She meant the comparison to be tongue-in-cheek, but Meg picked up on how alienated she really felt and clucked her tongue sympathetically.

"Do you want me to visit you this weekend? I work Friday and Sunday, but I could come for the day on Saturday."

"Oh, that's really sweet, but it's too far to drive for one day. I'll be fine. I think I'm feeling sorry for myself because I was just getting over Toby dumping me the way he did and then I came here only to face more rejection. If it wasn't that Ivan's going to need extended care when he comes home, I'd be tempted to leave sooner rather than later."

"Yeah, he's going to have a long recovery," Meg acknowledged. "Have you told them at work you won't be coming back for a while?"

"I'll let them know at the end of the week. I dread making that call, though."

"Why? You can legitimately take family medical leave."

"Yeah, but only the people in human resources will know *why* I'm taking a leave of absence. Everyone else is going to assume I'm heartbroken because of Toby and Brianna." Rachel recognized she shouldn't care what they thought, but it still bugged her to imagine anyone pitying her, especially Toby. *Wait until I get accepted into the MSN program and quit my position at the clinic—then they'll see I'm not as naive or needy as they think I am.* "Anyway, if you run out of clothes, feel free to borrow some from my closet. It's not as if I'll be using them any time soon."

After she said goodbye to Meg, Rachel realized she should do a load of laundry herself, especially since she had a thick smudge of lavender paint down the front of her navy blue skirt, and in addition to her green skirt, she'd only brought one other dress. *It's either I wash my clothes in the wringer tomorrow morning or I sew new ones.*

Thinking about sewing reminded Rachel of the time Toby and his younger brother, also a doctor, had held a contest to determine whose suturing technique was better. They each cut the skin of a grape and then sutured it closed again to present to their father, an orthopedic surgeon, for him to judge. Watching them, Rachel decided to give it a try, too. When Dr. Grand Sr. saw the results of her attempt, he declared *her* the winner. She credited all the time she spent quilting, as well as sewing capes, aprons and dresses, for her coordination and steady hand.

Suddenly it occurred to Rachel that she'd be expected to suture patients' wounds once she became a nurse practitioner, and she decided to stop by the local fabric store at her next opportunity. Not only would sewing a skirt or two give her more wardrobe choices, but it would allow her the chance to improve her manual dexterity for the future. *Who needs visitors anyway?* she asked herself. *In a little while, Ivan will be coming home, and I'll have his company. Meanwhile, I'll keep myself busy by focusing on what's really important—preparing for my career as a nurse practitioner.*

"*Mamm*'s fingers seem to be getting worse," Grace said as she set a box of cereal in front of Arden on Thursday morning. Usually, she made a big breakfast, but she'd woken up late; she'd probably been up most of the night, trying to keep their mother hydrated and her fever down. "I really think we should ask Rachel if she'll take a look at them."

"*Neh*, I've already told you that's not a *gut* idea," Arden objected. He shook the box above his bowl, and only a half cup of grain poured out. It didn't matter; his sister always sent him off with a hearty lunch, and he could take his break earlier than usual.

"Why not? You just told me you're so busy at the shop you have to work until seven thirty again tonight and tomorrow evening. If Rachel takes a peek at *Mamm*'s hands and says it's nothing serious, it would spare you from taking time off to bring her to the *dokder*."

Arden's sister had her own horse and buggy to use for running errands nearby, but she was nervous about driving to the hillier, western section of town where the medical clinic their mother went to was located. The *Englischers* in Serenity Ridge, while respectful, weren't as cautious as the *Englisch* drivers in Indiana, who were accustomed to slowing their vehicles as they crested hills, never knowing if a buggy was just out of sight and traveling at a much slower pace on the descending side. More than once since she moved to Maine, Grace had experienced a car approaching her too quickly from behind, which not only spooked the horse but frightened Grace to the point she was unwilling to travel to the clinic unless absolutely necessary. So it was up to Arden to either transport his mother to her medical appointments or arrange for a cab or someone in the district to take her.

He silently dithered over what to do. Grace was right; he could ill afford to take time away from the workshop, especially since yesterday he'd accepted a rush order—something he virtually never did, but it was only for a chicken coop, and the customer was willing to pay handsomely for the inconvenience of the short notice. However, his sister had also told him their mother was experiencing a strange discoloration of the skin on her fingers. Although her lupus flares primarily included a classic butterfly rash on her face, extreme fatigue and a chronic fever, their mother been advised to seek medical attention for any new symptoms. She'd said the discoloration didn't last long and wasn't painful, but Arden didn't want to take any chances.

"I understand you don't want Rachel coming to the house for a social visit, but this would be for medical purposes only," Grace said. "We could compensate her for her trouble, if that's what you're worried about."

"*Neh*, that's not it. It's that… It's that Rachel is only a nurse, not a *dokder*. I want *Mamm* to get the best care. I'll use the work phone to schedule an appointment for her at the clinic. We'll figure out the transportation logistics once we know what time she has to be there."

"I'm not sick enough to go to the clinic. Grace worries too much," Oneita said as she shuffled into the kitchen with a water glass in her hand. "Next time I go to the rheumatologist, I'll tell him about my fingers. Who's Rachel?"

Pleased that Grace had honored Ivan's request not to tell anyone about Rachel, Arden ignored his mother's question. "Are you sure you're okay?"

"Jah," she answered and then was overtaken by a coughing fit. Grace hovered over her, wringing her hands. When Oneita stopped wheezing, she took a sip of water and then said, "I'm fine, but I need to lie down again. Would you make some white willow bark tea with a drop of honey, Grace? I think my fever is back."

Grace placed her hand over her mother's forehead. "*Jah*, you're *waarem*. I'll walk you to your room."

When she returned, Grace scowled at Arden and picked up their conversation right where they'd left off. "I don't understand you sometimes. If Rachel is anything like Ivan, she'll be *hallich* to help. Or is it that you're afraid *Mamm* and I won't be polite to her because she went *Englisch*? I promise we'll *wilkom* her into our home as warmly as we'd *wilkom* any Amish woman."

That was exactly what Arden was worried about. Once Grace and his mother got to chatting, there was no telling what they'd say to Rachel. *I've got enough on my mind without worrying whether they're going to try to convince an* Englischer *to take pity on a* dumm *Amish bachelor and* kumme *back to Serenity Ridge for* gut *so I can marry her.* "If *Mamm's* fingers get worse, call me on the business phone," he instructed his sister and bolted from the house.

It wasn't until ten thirty when he caught a glimpse of Rachel dipping a piece of a sticky bun into her coffee that Arden realized he'd forgotten the lunch his sister packed for him. His mouth watered. Rachel glanced up, and he hastily averted his eyes. For the past couple days, he'd been careful not to even comment about the weather in her presence, lest she take it as an invitation to strike up a longer conversation. She must have noticed him looking at her now and interpreted that as a sign he wanted to chat, because she dipped the last piece of the bun into her cup, popped the dripping morsel into her mouth and then sauntered in his direction as she licked a dab of icing from her upper lip. Arden's stomach growled. It was going to be a long day without any sustenance to tide him over.

"You're making *gut* progress," she said about the coop.

"*Jah*, but the customer wants to pick it up on Saturday, which means I need to finish building it by tomorrow morning or else the paint won't dry," he replied. He stammered when he added, "W-would you, uh, b-be willing to help?"

"*Me?*" Rachel's voice squeaked with disbelief. Arden knew he shouldn't have asked; when she'd volunteered to paint the playhouse, it was probably a onetime offer only.

"Nev-never mind. Y-you don't have to. I thought because you s-s-said there wasn't enough for you to do you wouldn't mind. And you did such a *g-gut* job painting the playhouse," he stuttered.

"Oh—you want me to *paint* it!" The tiny scar on Rachel's cheekbone leaped higher with her smile. "When you asked for my help, I thought you meant you wanted me to help you *build* the coop. I'm *hallich* to paint it—I'll do any work around here that doesn't involve swinging a hammer, using a saw or wielding a drill. What color does the customer want it painted?"

Delighted by Rachel's response, Arden grinned. "You'll never guess."

"Please don't say lavender."

"*Neh.* Guess again." Despite being pressed for time, Arden was in no hurry to have their conversation end.

She guessed turquoise, yellow and pink before giving up.

"Eggshell white." He kept a straight face as he waited for her reaction.

"Oh. White's no so bad—" she started to say before she got the joke. "*Egg*shell white for a chicken coop. *Voll schpass!*" When she tipped her head back in laughter, her hair spilled over her shoulders and down her back. Amish women sometimes wore their long hair loose at home in the evening, so Arden had seen locks of all different textures and colors, but never had he so closely beheld hair as lustrous as Rachel's. As she moved, he caught a whiff of coconut mingled with...almond? Hunger clawed at his stomach.

"Actually, the family wants red, like a barn. They wanted the inside painted, too. They claimed a dark color is more conducive for the hens to lay than natural wood, but that's where I drew the line. I don't have the time, and I'm concerned the chickens will end up pecking the paint off anyway. They were awfully disappointed when I said *neh.*"

"Who, the family or the poultry?" Rachel was tipping her head coyly to one side, clearly teasing him.

"Probably both." Arden was so at ease he didn't have to think about what to say or how to say it—his words and jokes were flowing readily.

"*Jah*, everyone knows what high expectations those *Englisch* chickens can have. You're just fortunate they didn't ask you to *wallpaper* the inside of their coop," she replied. When Arden stopped laughing, Rachel added, "I'm actually being serious. I know some *Englischers* who wallpapered the inside of their coops. They used vinyl wallpaper, like the kind people use to line their drawers, because they say it makes cleaning the coop a lot easier."

Arden shrugged. "That wouldn't be my choice, but if it's what they want to do, who am I to convince them otherwise?"

He picked up his hammer and got back to work, but inwardly he was savoring their exchange. It occurred to him Rachel not only had a terrific sense of humor, but her work ethic was as diligent as any Amish woman's he'd ever known. And most of those women would have chewed him out something fierce for ruining their paint job the way he'd ruined hers the other day, but she found it comical. *Colin is too hard on her*, Arden realized once again. *Rachel might not be Amish anymore, but she's a* gut *woman.*

Who knew taciturn Arden could be so humorous? Rachel swallowed the rest of her lukewarm coffee and set the cup back on her desk. She was glad to have another painting project to complete, and now that Arden was warming up to her again, she hoped things around the workshop wouldn't continue to be so dreadfully dull.

After taking a quick peek at her phone to confirm she hadn't received an email from the MSN program yet, Rachel spent the rest of the morning rechecking the figures in the ledger. One of the few comments Arden had made to her on Tuesday was that he was concerned there might not be enough funds in the business account to cover Ivan's hospital bill. But after reviewing the ledger twice, Rachel was confident they could withdraw the amount in full and still have a few thousand dollars left over.

She was about to break for lunch when a tall, red-headed *Englischer* entered the shop and introduced himself as Chris Jones, the hardware and tool supplier for the business. There was something familiar about him, but he didn't show any sign of recognition when Rachel told him her name, so she concluded she must have seen him in passing at the grocery store or maybe in church on Sunday.

"I was on my way to Unity, so I thought I'd deliver these since they were special order so we couldn't pack them with the supplies they received last week. Seemed kind of silly for Ivan or Arden to hitch up the buggy and come all the way to the store for a single box of nails."

"That was thoughtful. If you give me a moment, I'll pay you for the entire order. I just saw that invoice," Rachel suggested. When she located the paperwork and finished writing out the check, she lifted her head to find Chris studying her intently.

He immediately apologized. "I don't mean to stare, but I feel like we've met before."

"So do I but I don't know whe—wait, Chris Jones.

You're Paige Jones's brother!" His surname hadn't registered with her right away, because it was so common.

"Ah, you're one of Paige's friends." The crease across his forehead indicated Chris still couldn't place Rachel.

"Sort of. She tutored me ten years ago when I was studying to get my GED. We met at your house, and your parents often invited me to stay for supper. I think I only met you once or twice when you were home from college for the holidays," Rachel explained.

Chris palmed his forehead. "How could I forget? Paige talked about you all the time. She said you were a really quick learner and you caught on to everything right away."

Rachel briskly shook her head. "If that's true, it's because Paige was such an effective teacher. I lost touch with her years ago. What's she doing now?"

"Teaching, of course. On a reservation in New Mexico."

"I'm not surprised. She had a keen interest in connecting with people whose cultures are different from her own. So did your parents. They were intrigued by my Amish background." Rachel stole a glance in Arden's direction. His back was turned as he searched the shelves along the wall, but she felt self-conscious, worrying whether he was within earshot. She could understand why it might be considered disrespectful for her to stand in the presence of an Amish person and casually chat with an *Englischer* about her decision to leave the community. She didn't want to offend Arden, but neither did Rachel want to cut her conversation with Chris short, considering his sister had been instrumental in helping her.

"So, did you, er, decide to stay after all?"

Rachel giggled softly; she could imagine how confusing it was for Chris to see her working in an Amish shop dressed as an *Englischer*, especially considering the last he knew, she was planning to leave the Amish. "No, after I got my GED, I moved to Boston, went to college and became an RN. And right now, I'm waiting to hear if I've been accepted to an MSN program to become a nurse practitioner." Then, to further clarify, she added, "Ivan's my brother and he's been in the hospital with pneumonia, so I'm only in Serenity Ridge temporarily to help out."

Chris congratulated her on her academic and career successes before saying, "I had no idea you were related to Ivan. That's too bad he's been so sick. Your family is fortunate to have you here."

I wish they *felt that way.* "Please give Paige my fond regards when you speak to her. And greet your parents for me, as well."

Once Chris was gone, Rachel sat down again and mindlessly filed away the invoice, but her thoughts harkened back to the evenings she'd spent conversing with Paige and her parents. They'd been nonjudgmental as they listened to Rachel ponder aloud the pros and cons of leaving her Amish family and community, neither encouraging her to go nor persuading her to stay, even when she was so conflicted she begged Mrs. Jones to tell her what she should do.

"I think you should keep praying for wisdom," Mrs. Jones had responded. Rachel had been hoping for a more definitive answer, but when she pushed for one, Mrs. Jones merely added, "It might help to remember whether you choose to leave or stay you can always change your mind later if you believe God is leading you in a different direction."

I can't imagine ever living here permanently again, Rachel mused. Then she spied Arden's broad shoulders as he stood in front of the supply shelf, and as she reflected on their playful morning banter, she smiled and thought, *But I suppose visiting isn't so bad after all.*

Arden slid the box of hinges—they weren't what he was looking for—back into its slot among the other boxes of nails, screws, nuts and bolts. He hadn't been able to keep from overhearing Rachel and Chris talking, and their conversation had distracted him and dampened his sunny mood. While he was disconcerted to discover their trusty hardware supplier's family had helped Rachel leave the Amish a decade ago, he was even more dismayed to learn about Rachel's career plans. *Why should I be surprised she has ambitions to become a nurse practitioner?* he asked himself.

No, Rachel wasn't as haughty as she was rumored to be—nor was she even as snooty as Arden's initial impression of her. In fact, when Chris complimented her for being a quick learner, Arden noticed Rachel had deflected his praise; she'd demonstrated *demut,* or humility, the opposite of *hochmut.* But as Rachel's goals for the future demonstrated, she had an insatiable appetite for knowledge. *She may be Ivan's sister, she may be a hard worker and she may be schpass, but I'd do well to remember she's still an* Englischer. *A very* schmaert *one at that.*

"I'm going to go eat now." Rachel's voice cut into Arden's thoughts. Although they routinely took their lunch break at the same time, she went to the house to eat while he ate in the workshop or outside on the bench beneath a peach tree. "How about you? It's nearly one thirty."

"I'm working through lunch today," he answered, although the very word *lunch* made his stomach raw.

"You can't go without eating. You'll get a *koppweh*," she warned. "Trust me, I know these things. I'm a nurse."

As if I could forget. "A nurse, soon to be a nurse practitioner," he muttered.

"You heard me tell Chris that?" Rachel cocked her head.

Intending to clarify that he hadn't been eavesdropping, Arden said, "It would have been hard not to. This is an open space with high ceilings. If it was a secret, you should have lowered your voice."

"I have nothing to hide." Rachel sounded insulted, and Arden realized he'd been too gruff. Maybe she was right; he was getting peckish.

"Not even the 5/32-inch wood screws?" he ribbed, trying too late to make her smile. "I thought we had half a box left."

"They're right in front of you." She was already turning on her heel.

"Where? I don't see them."

She pivoted around again and pointed. "If the box gets any closer, it's going to bite you in the nose— 532WS. Read the product code."

Arden lifted his hand midway to the shelf, but he still didn't see which box she meant. What was the code again? He and Ivan never paid attention to codes— they'd arranged the hardware according to what they used most often, and Arden had memorized where every last item was located on the shelves. He touched the box he thought the screws were in and Rachel tugged his sleeve to move his hand away.

"Are you putting me on or do you seriously need glasses? Those ending in *DWS* are the drywall screws, not wood screws." She reached in front of him to remove a box from the shelf near his opposite shoulder.

"Aha, when you said nose level, you meant *your* nose level, not mine." He tried to cover his mistake with humor, but it was lost on her as she hurried toward the door. His hand must have been shaky from hunger, because the box slipped from his fingers, spraying screws across the floor. He was squatting to pick them up when the door opened and in walked Grace. Arden's heart raced, but before he could ask her, she assured him their mother was fine.

"Anke Beiler came by to *qwilde* with her. *Mamm*'s not ready for that yet, but the white willow bark tea she drank must have helped a lot, because her fever is gone. Anyway, Anke said she'd stay there and visit so I could run a few errands, including bringing you your lunch."

"*Denki*. You didn't have to do that, but I'm glad you did." Arden realized sometimes he was so stressed out about what was happening at the workshop he didn't thank his sister often enough for all she did to care for their mother and keep the household running smoothly.

"It's okay. It was on my way to the fabric shop." Looking around, Grace casually inquired, "So, where's Rachel today?"

"She's up at the *haus* eating lunch."

The words had barely left his mouth when Rachel burst through the door. "I forgot my phone," she announced breathlessly as she swiped it off the desk. It must have taken a moment for her to register Grace's presence, because Rachel came to an abrupt halt. Single-handedly gathering her hair and holding it against the nape of her neck, she stuttered, "H-hello."

"Hello. You must be Rachel. I'm Arden's sister, Grace."

Rachel immediately dropped her hand, and her hair swung free as a smile illuminated her features, from forehead to chin. She squeezed Grace's arm. "It's so nice to meet you, Grace! *Denki* for the meal you brought the other day. It was *appenditlich*."

"I'm glad you enjoyed it. I'm actually delivering Arden a meal today, too." Grace impishly put her hand to the opposite side of her mouth, pretending to whisper behind it, "He forgot his lunch, and he gets cranky when he doesn't eat."

"Oh, that explains a lot," Rachel joked. Or maybe she wasn't joking—Arden couldn't tell, but hearing how quickly Grace and Rachel teamed up to tease him made him uneasy.

"Grace is on her way to the fabric shop," he told Rachel, cupping his sister's elbow. "I'll walk you back to the buggy."

"I'm in no hurry." Grace planted her feet where she stood. "How is Ivan, Rachel?"

"He's getting a little stronger every day. He'll probably *kumme* home this weekend," Rachel said. "But if you'd like to go visit him in the hos—"

Arden cut her off. "Grace, you're keeping Rachel from her lunch. She has to go now."

Grace raised an eyebrow at him before addressing Rachel, whose cheeks were flushed. "You'll have to forgive my *bruder* for interrupting you. Not only does he become irritable when he's *hungerich*, but he forgets his manners, too."

"It's okay, I understand. That's what happens when someone's blood sugar drops too low. You really ought to eat now, Arden," Rachel advised. She sounded so genuinely concerned Arden felt bad for having interrupted her like he did—until she turned to Grace and said, "You know, I was planning to go to the fabric store, too. How about if we go together?"

"Perfect! It will give us a chance to get better acquainted."

Now Arden was really desperate. "Y-y-you're going to be gone that long, Rachel? What if a cu-customer calls?"

"I'll take the business phone with me," Rachel told him. To Grace she added, "But he's right, it might take more time than I can spare if we travel by buggy. Are you comfortable going in my car?"

"Sure, as long as I don't have to drive," Grace said, giggling.

Arden must have appeared as apprehensive as he felt, because when Rachel looked at him she said, "Are you sure you're going to be okay? You look peaked."

"*Jah*, once I have lunch, I'll be fine," he resigned himself to saying, even though he was no longer the least bit hungry.

Chapter Five

"You sound a lot happier tonight," Meg said a few minutes after Rachel called Thursday night on her speakerphone as she drove home from visiting Ivan. "Did you find out you got into the MSN program?"

Rachel groaned. "I'm sorry I've been so moody lately, but you're right, I do feel a lot happier tonight, and no, it's not because I found out anything about my application. It's because I had a *gut* afternoon at the fabric store with Arden's *schweschder*, Grace."

Meg cracked up, and when Rachel asked what was so funny, she imitated, "A *gut* afternoon with Arden's *schweschder*. You're sounding more and more Amish every day."

Rachel laughed, too. "If you think I *sound* Amish, wait till you see how Amish I look in the dress I'm making."

"What?" Meg's tone suddenly changed. "Why are you making Amish clothes? You're going to stay there permanently, aren't you?"

"Don't be *lecher*—ridiculous. I'm making a dress

because I brought so few skirts, and it gives me something to do in the evenings until Ivan is discharged."

"Sewing doesn't sound like a fun way to spend an evening. Haven't you met any handsome, eligible bachelors who could take you out?"

"Only Arden." Rachel's answer slipped out of her mouth before she realized how it sounded. "I mean, he's the only bachelor I've met, and his sister told me he's not courting anyone. Which obviously is neither here nor there, because he's Amish. My point is, no, I haven't met any eligible bachelors I'd consider going out with." She was grateful Meg couldn't see her face, because her cheeks felt aflame.

"For as much as you've told me about Arden, you've never told me what he looks like. Is he handsome?"

"Not that it matters, but yeah, I suppose he's good-looking. He's tall and has blond—blond*ish*—curls and light blue eyes. And a nice smile, when he smiles, which is rare."

"He's still being Mr. Morose?"

"Well…sometimes. It's hard to say. He sort of turns on a dime. Like this morning, he was cracking jokes right and left, and then all of a sudden, he became surly again because I was talking too loudly to a customer or he couldn't find where I put the inventory. And when his sister came by, he all but tried to drag her out of the workshop rather than let her talk to me. Who knows, maybe he's afraid I'll be a bad influence on her and she'll go *Englisch*, too."

"But she's friendly to you?"

"Very. Although I suspect part of that is because she's interested in my brother."

"But you're not interested in *her* brother?"

"Not at all," Rachel insisted. "He's Amish, remember?"

"*I* remember. Do *you* remember?"

Rachel gave an exaggerated huff. "Just for that, I'm saying goodbye now, Meg."

"*Gut nacht,*" Meg chirped, and they both laughed before hanging up.

I don't know why she'd suggest I'm romantically interested in Arden, Rachel thought. *I think she's just being* lappich *on purpose, to amuse me. The idea is as* narrish *as the thought of me lingering in Serenity Ridge. The moment Ivan is well again, I'm out of here.*

Meanwhile, she was glad she'd gone to the fabric store with Grace, who'd filled her in on the news in Serenity Ridge. Ivan rarely mentioned people other than their family members when he wrote to Rachel, so she was surprised to discover how the population had grown and changed since she'd lived there. The fledgling community was only a little over twenty years old, and already it had nearly tripled in size, despite the fact several of the people who originally settled there had either returned to their home states, married and moved away, or passed on.

Maybe I'm being too sensitive to think people are avoiding me—they might not even live here any longer, Rachel realized. *I suppose* I *could try to introduce myself to the Amish. But how?* Showing up at church after having been gone for ten years would likely be awkward for everyone, as would dropping in on someone she used to know. And she wasn't about to attend a singing. Ah well—for tonight she literally had her work cut out for her; she'd purchased fabric in a bright spring color Grace said would look pretty with her hair and eyes. It wasn't until she'd already cut into it that she realized she'd chosen almost the exact shade of lavender Arden had spilled inside the playhouse, and the recollection made her laugh all over again.

"Arden, *kumme* look at this," Grace called from the living room when he walked through the door on Thursday evening. It was after eight o'clock and he was beat, but hearing the urgency in his sister's voice, he raced through the kitchen without removing his muddy boots.

She was standing over their mother, who was reclining on the sofa in a housecoat. "Stop fussing," Oneita said to Grace. "Let your *bruder* eat his supper."

Grace wouldn't listen. "Look at *Mamm*'s fingers, Arden. *That's* what I've been telling you keeps happening. Please show him, *Mamm*."

Oneita sighed, but she held up her hands. Although her thumbs were spared, the top halves of all eight of her fingers were so white they nearly glowed.

"Do they hurt?"

"They tingle a little, like when your foot falls asleep, but they don't hurt."

"Were you leaning on them?"

"*Neh.* I just got out of the tub."

Arden tugged at his ear. "Did you use a new soap or something?"

"What is this, twenty questions?" Grace snapped. "She didn't *do* anything. It just happens. See—now they're turning blue. This is the sequence it follows. It's not going to do us any *gut* to guess what's happening. We need a medical professional's help."

"But if it doesn't really hurt..." Oneita said, even as she winced and wiggled her fingers.

"*Mamm*, there might be an underlying reason this is

happening. If that's the case, it needs to be addressed now, before it progresses. I don't want you to end up suffering needlessly." Grace's tone indicated she was struggling to remain patient. She shot a look at Arden and added, "The longer we wait, the more expensive the treatment might be."

Although money might have been a prohibitive issue a few days ago, it was no longer Arden's primary consideration. Thank the Lord, his concern over Ivan's hospital bill had finally been put to rest this afternoon when Rachel confirmed she'd combed through the ledger, checking and rechecking the figures, and she'd assured him they had money to spare, even if Ivan wasn't discharged on Saturday or Sunday as expected. Arden didn't quite know how to explain their extra funds, but who was he to doubt Rachel? She'd carefully tracked every bill paid, supply bought and delivery scheduled and insisted they were in the black.

What he was more concerned about now was meeting the deadlines for the projects he'd taken on in an attempt to bring in as much money as possible during Ivan's hospitalization. He was already working from six thirty in the morning until seven thirty or eight o'clock each evening. He hadn't even begun the shed that was scheduled for pickup on Monday and he couldn't work on the Sabbath, so how could he take time off to bring his mother to the clinic? Granted, he or Grace could ask someone else to take her, but there was no guarantee anyone would be available. Oneita taking a cab was even less likely than Grace taking the buggy to that side of town; cabs made her nervous, and she'd only ride in one if absolutely necessary.

"Has it gotten worse or happened more frequently?" Arden asked his mother.

"*Neh*. Definitely not."

Grace threw her hands in the air. "Arden! Are you going to wait until her fingers fall off to do anything about this?" She stormed from the room, and Arden rubbed his eyes, stupefied by her comment.

His mother merely chuckled. "Don't listen to her, Arden. If my fingers fall off, we'll sew them back on again."

Arden didn't find the thought amusing. He sank into a cushion at the opposite end of the sofa. "Grace is right, *Mamm*. We need to get this checked out sooner rather than later. I'm sorry I hesitated. It wasn't that I don't want to take the time or spend the money. You're more than worth it. It's…" He stopped speaking, realizing if his mother's health truly was his priority, he wouldn't offer the flimsy excuse of needing to meet his work commitments.

"I know, *suh*." His mother leaned forward to pat his knee. "You're shouldering a lot of responsibility at the workshop—more than usual. That's important not just for the customers, but for you and your *familye*, and especially for Ivan. Unless my hands get worse, this can wait."

"*Neh—*"

His mother pointed a finger at him; it had almost returned to its normal hue. "You and your *schweschder* take excellent care of me and I appreciate it, but I am still your *mamm* and this is still my body, so I'm making this decision, not you. I'll tell my rheumatologist about my fingers at my next appointment."

Arden shook his head. "Can we compromise? Since

I have a shed due on Monday, I'll schedule an appointment for you for Tuesday. If your hands get better before then, we'll cancel it. But if they get worse, we'll go to the *dokder* immediately."

"All right, all right. But the only reason I'm agreeing to this is because otherwise Grace is going to be upset with you."

"*Jah.* Remember the time I procrastinated installing a heater in her buggy and she served meat loaf every night until I got around to doing it?" Meat loaf was Arden's least favorite food.

"Do I ever! Even *I* didn't like meat loaf anymore after that," his mother joked. "And if we don't want it for supper tomorrow night, you'd better wipe up the floor. Look at that mud."

Arden gamely went into the kitchen to take off his boots and wipe up the footprints before returning to the living room to mop the floor there, too. As he worked, his mother said, "I'm surprised Grace flew off the handle tonight. She came back from the fabric store in such a *gut* mood."

"Oh?" Arden didn't look up from wringing the cloth into the bucket. Rachel had seemed almost giddy after the trip to the fabric store, too. All afternoon he'd had to fight the temptation to worry about whether Grace told Rachel something he wouldn't have wanted her to disclose, such as that he had trouble reading or that their *mamm* wished he'd meet someone to court.

"*Jah*, she said Ivan's *schweschder* took her in her car—don't fret, she made me promise I wouldn't tell anyone Rachel is here, although I can't imagine it will stay a secret for very long. Anyway, afterward they drove around so Grace could show Rachel some of the new farms and Amish *heiser* in Serenity Ridge."

That would explain why they were gone so long. "Hmm."

"Grace said Rachel is in her late twenties. There aren't too many people that age to socialize with here. You ought to invite her to our *haus* for supper after work one evening."

I knew that was coming, Arden thought. *I wish the weather were as predictable as my* mamm *and* schweschder. "She goes to visit Ivan in the evenings after work."

"Ah, that's right. She offered Grace a ride. I'm surprised she didn't offer to take you, too, considering your relationship with Ivan."

"She did offer, *Mamm.*" Arden shifted himself upright and picked up the bucket.

"But you didn't accept? Don't the two of you get along? Or are you uncomfortable about how it would appear to be alone with her? If that's it, Grace could go with you, too."

Arden felt trapped; no matter what he said, his mother would likely draw the wrong conclusion. "W-we wo-work w-well together." The repetition of *W*s made his stutter even more pronounced. He edged toward the door, adding, "I-I've b-been working late and I wa-wanted to give her time alone with her *br-bruder* since it's been so long since she's seen him. She went *Englisch* ten years ago, you know. She hasn't been b-back since then."

"*Jah,* Grace mentioned that." A frown pulled at his mother's mouth. Satisfied she'd gotten the message, Arden moved toward the kitchen on his way to dump the dirty water outside. Just as he turned the door handle, his mother called, "When Ivan comes home from the hospital, we'll have to invite both him and Rachel to have supper with us. Won't that be *schpass*?"

Rachel kicked her sheet aside. Between the rainy weather and the warming temperatures, there was already a hint of summer humidity in the air. It was a good thing she could sew quickly, because if the heat kept up, she couldn't continue to wear the clothing she'd brought with her, with the exception of the short-sleeved cotton top she planned to put on again today.

The clamminess in the air not only made her cranky, it caused her hair to wilt, too, so she swept it into a high ponytail. It felt good to have it off her neck, but Rachel realized if she leaned forward while she was painting the chicken coop, her ponytail might brush against it and she'd wind up with even redder highlights than her natural ones. She released her hair and gathered it in a bun at the nape of her neck instead. *I can imagine what Meg would say if she saw me now...*

The rain was coming down in sheets as she sprinted across the lawn to the workshop a few minutes later. The instant she reached the door, she realized she'd left her cell phone at the house and had to race back. The battery was running low—she didn't drive often enough to keep it charged—but it had enough power for her to check her email for news from the university. The second time she got to the workshop, she was so soaked she felt as if she'd been swimming.

"Guder mariye," Arden greeted her from behind the wall of a shed that hadn't been there when she'd left the previous evening. He was *fast*.

"Guder mariye," she echoed. Noticing she was dripping on the catalogs on the desk, she asked, "Do we have any towels in here?"

"Neh," Arden replied as he came around the shed into view. He did a double take when he spotted her. "The rags in the bin are clean, though. Let me get you a couple."

"Denki," she said when he handed her several cloths in assorted sizes a moment later. She patted one along the length of her sleeves before using the second one to blot her hair and then her face. Lowering the cloth, she spied Arden watching her. "I know, I look like a drowned rat."

His ears turned pink. "D-do you wa-want me to run to the *haus* and get a r-real towel?"

"If you do, it'll be wet before you make it halfway back to the fence," she replied. "Just listen to it coming down." They both paused and looked toward the roof of the barn, which was being pelted with raindrops. "Even *you* don't make that much noise when you're hammering, and you've got a really quick, powerful swing," Rachel said.

When Arden's cheeks and neck ignited with color, Rachel realized her comment may have sounded flirtatious, but she didn't know how to indicate that wasn't her intention. Changing the subject, she said, "I guess if there's one *gut* thing about wearing my hair like this, it's that it doesn't look any different when it's wet than when it's dry."

Terrific, now it sounded as if she was insulting Amish women's hairstyles. Rachel didn't know what was wrong with her brain and mouth today, but they weren't doing her any favors. "Ivan really should keep an umbrella in the *haus*," she added feebly.

"I suppose he figures since he wears a hat, he doesn't need an umbrella," Arden remarked with a shrug, and Rachel was glad he walked away before she could embarrass either of them again.

As Arden pulled out his tape measure and measured the length of a joist, he fought to keep his hands steady. Ordinarily, he might have felt complimented if a young woman noticed his strength, but coming from Rachel, it unnerved him.

But why? Because she's Englisch? he asked himself. She sure didn't look *Englisch* today; with her hair combed into a bun like that, for the first time Arden could envision the young Amish girl she'd been before she left Serenity Ridge. The severe hairstyle was an unsettling contrast with her *Englisch* clothing, and he wished she'd worn her tresses loose, the way she usually did, but that was beside the point. It wasn't her hair or clothing or the fact she'd gone *Englisch* that made him feel upset by her flattery. Arden was upset because he realized a comment about his strength was going to be the best compliment he'd ever get from Rachel. *It's not as if someone that bright would ever think of me as clever or wise.*

His tape measure snapped his thumb as he retracted it into its casing; he had the reflexes of an amateur this morning. Last night he'd lain awake in bed for hours, worrying about his mother and Grace eventually inviting Ivan and Rachel to supper. Board games would inevitably follow their meal, and if any of those games involved reading aloud... Arden yawned. He was tired.

Tired from having spent the night tossing and turning, tired from trying to stay one step ahead of their customers, and tired from trying to hide his shortcomings. How ironic that the one thing people noticed about him was his strength, when at the moment, he felt as weary as could be. He closed his eyes and prayed. *Lord, please empower me to do Your will today and to meet the commitments I've made to others.*

"Arden? Are you okay?"

His eyes flew open; Rachel stood in front of him. "*Jah.* Do you need something?"

She extended him the phone. "Grace wants to talk to you. She sounds upset."

He pressed the phone to his ear. "What's wrong, Grace?"

"It's *Mamm*'s…this time it's not just…and her…" Whether it was because of the rain, the phone shanty or the cell phone's reception, Grace's voice kept cutting in and out.

"I can't hear you, Grace. But I'm coming home right away. I'm bringing Rachel. We'll be right there." He turned toward the desk to ask Rachel for her help, but as he'd mentioned the day before, sound carried well in the workshop and she'd heard everything he'd said.

"I'll run to the *haus* to get my keys. You lock up here and meet me at the car."

Reaching the car before Rachel did, Arden prayed, *Please, Gott, keep Mamm well.*

A moment later Rachel slid into the seat behind the steering wheel. "Which road do I take?" she asked as they neared the end of the driveway.

Arden's mind clouded, and his tongue felt thick. Two of the three streets he usually traveled to access the road he lived on were washed out, so he'd taken a roundabout way to the workshop that morning. He couldn't have told Rachel the names of those streets if his life depended on it—not even if his *mother's* life depended on it.

"Arden." Her voice was firm but calm. "Which way?"

"R-r-right," he said, and she turned in the opposite direction of where he wanted her to go.

He hadn't mixed up right and left for years—it only happened when he was stressed or tired. As a child, it had taken him much longer than the other students to learn the concept of right and left. He was finally able to memorize the two directions when the teacher told him, "Think of it this way. *Right* is on the same side as the hand I *write* with. The other hand is left." Except Arden always completed the mnemonic as, "The other hand is wrong."

"Neh!" he barked now. "Wrong! Go wrong!"

Rachel tapped the brake, and his upper torso swung toward the dashboard before the seat belt jerked his momentum to a stop. "Which way do you want me to go? Right or left?"

Arden pointed. "That way."

"Okay." She reached over and tapped his hand, repeating, "Okay. It's going to be okay."

For the rest of their trip, each time they came to a stop sign or the end of a street, he'd squint into the rain and point in the direction he wanted her to continue. The downpour pelted the rooftop so hard it made it difficult for them to hear each other, and twice they temporarily lost all visibility when passing vehicles shrouded them in water.

"Ivan told me about your *Mamm's* lupus. Has she had

a flare of symptoms recently?" Rachel asked as they approached another four-way stop.

"*Jah*, a fe-fever." Arden pointed. "Up the hill. Then t-turn by the *Grischtdaag* tree farm."

Rachel did as he said. "Anything else?"

Arden was confused; couldn't she see the tree farm? "There's a small b-barn."

"No, I meant any other symptoms?"

"She's tired. And her ha-hands are—" He rapidly tapped the dashboard. "Here, turn here. Down this road at the end is wh-where I live."

"Hold on, I haven't stopped the car yet," Rachel said when she pulled up to the house, but Arden already had one leg out the door. How many times had she treated patients who'd wound up injured because they'd panicked while trying to help a family member during an emergency?

She turned off the ignition, nabbed her first aid kit from beneath the seat and hurried behind him into the house, through the kitchen and into the living room. There a thin, older woman whose head of dark hair didn't contain a strand of gray was placidly resting in an armchair while Grace stood beside her holding a glass of water.

"Why, hello. You must be Rachel Blank. I'm Oneita Esh," the woman greeted her as if she'd been expecting Rachel to stop by for a sister day.

Before Rachel could respond, Arden began firing off questions. "Are you okay, *Mamm*? Is it your hands? Grace, what happened?"

"Her nose changed color, just like her fingers. It was the oddest thing."

Oneita looked at Rachel and raised her hands as she shrugged. "They're better now, as you can see. I only wanted Grace to tell Arden we might need to schedule an appointment after all, but I guess they didn't have a *gut* phone connection. I'm sorry you came all the way out here in the rain. Grace—please make Rachel a cup of tea. She's dripping wet."

"*Mamm*, as long as we're here, you should let Rachel look at your hands. And your nose," Arden suggested.

Oneita rolled her eyes. "My *kinner* fret so much you'd think *they're* the *eldre* and *I'm* the *kind*."

Rachel laughed. Then, sensing Arden and Grace's frustration with their mother, as well as Oneita's resistance, she suggested, "A cup of tea would be *wunderbaar*, Grace. Perhaps while you're making it and I'm chatting with your *mamm*, Arden will go remove his shoes and get a towel for me. I'm afraid we've made a mess of your floor."

Arden looked at her askance, but Grace sighed and nudged him out of the room, saying, "Okay, we'll give you privacy to chat."

"You're going to want to look me over, aren't you?" Oneita asked.

"It might help keep those two from breathing down your neck," Rachel whispered, causing Oneita to chuckle.

She proceeded to take Oneita's temperature and discuss her symptoms. Rachel was almost certain she could identify the phenomenon, as she'd read about it and seen several lupus patients treated for it in the clinic over the years. She didn't think Oneita's case was urgent, but since Rachel wasn't qualified to offer a diagnosis, she encouraged her to see a doctor soon.

As Arden and Grace reentered the room, Oneita argued, "I understand that, but I'd still like to hear what you think it is and what I can do about it until I get in for an appointment."

"*Mamm*, if she doesn't know for sure—" Arden started to say.

"She *does* know. And she knows what I can do to treat it or prevent it." Oneita pointed her finger at Rachel in a way that reminded her of her own mother. "*Kumme* now, you've studied and learned a lot about *Englisch* medicine. I understand some people might think that's a matter of *hochmut*. But it's false *hochmut* to act as if you don't know something when you clearly do."

Flustered, Rachel was at a momentary loss. Somehow Oneita's words sounded less like a scolding and more like…like *encouragement*. She felt the same way now that she'd felt when Arden pointed out how she'd held her ground with Colin—it was as if Oneita and Arden appreciated the very attributes in Rachel that the people in her family condemned as character flaws.

"Okay," she agreed. "I'll tell you what I know, but first I have to admit there's something that's confusing me. If this is what I think it is, usually it's triggered by cold temperatures, but the weather's been so warm lately. It seems odd you'd be experiencing it now—especially after bathing."

Grace clasped her hands together. "*Mamm*'s been taking tepid baths, not hot baths. It's what she does for her fever."

"But she didn't have a bath this morning, did she?" Arden countered. "And even if she did, it's not as if she put her nose under water."

"Maybe today was an exception," Oneita said.

"Did you do anything else with cold water today, *Mamm*?" Arden pressed. "Rinse vegetables? Make lemonade?"

"*Neh.* Grace has been doing all the food preparation. She thinks I'm so weak she barely allowed me to get my compress from the freezer before she was chasing me out again."

"*Mamm*, that's it! You opened the freezer, which is right at nose level, and you've been handling the compress. Could being exposed to the cold for such a short time trigger it, Rachel?"

"*Jah.* I think you've solved the mystery, Arden," Rachel said, silently admonishing herself for making assumptions about Oneita taking hot baths and for not asking additional questions, as Arden had done. But now that she was more confident about the diagnosis, she told the Eshes everything she knew about the disease, including how to prevent it, what to do when it happened, what tests the doctor might want to run and what alternative medicine options she might consider. She concluded by again urging Oneita to schedule a doctor's appointment.

"Arden will do that for me, but I doubt the *dokder* will tell me anything you haven't already said." Oneita brought her teacup to her lips. "Oh, this is cold. Would you put another kettle on for us, Grace?"

"Actually, Rachel and I ought to get back to the workshop now." Arden was shifting from foot to foot, but Rachel noticed the color had returned to his cheeks and he wasn't stuttering anymore. He was probably nervous about meeting his deadlines, and she didn't want to add to his anxiety.

"*Jah*, we should go," she agreed, hoping she didn't appear rude for dashing off.

"Then you must *kumme* for tea another day, shouldn't she, Grace?"

"Absolutely." Grace smiled at her brother. "Arden and I have been talking about Rachel visiting since she got here, haven't we, Arden?"

"*Denki*, I'd like that," Rachel agreed, and in that moment she realized just how much she'd longed to be welcomed into an Amish family's home again.

On the return trip, Arden could hardly speak, except to indicate in which direction Rachel should turn. Now that he wasn't so distraught over his mother's condition, he had the wherewithal to verbalize left or right instead of just pointing, but beyond that, speech eluded him. He needed to process the gamut of emotions he'd just experienced, from his fear about his mother's health to his admiration of how skillfully Rachel managed the situation, to his apprehension about her coming to their house socially. Fortunately, either Rachel understood his need for silence or she was deep in thought, too, because she was as quiet as he was.

Although the rain had let up and Rachel only used her intermittent wipers to clear a fine mist from the windshield, the unpaved back roads were soft with puddles. More than once she navigated onto the shoulder in order to bypass the standing water, but when they came to a particularly large pool that extended across the road's width, she stopped the car and bit her lip.

"Uh-oh. That looks deep. I better not cross it. I don't want the engine to seize." She glanced into the rearview mirror and at both sides of the road. "It's too narrow to turn here. I'm going to have to back up a little first, and then I can maneuver a three-point turn."

Rachel put the car into Reverse and Arden could hear the engine revving, but they went nowhere. "Are we stuck?"

"I think so. I'll look." Rachel shifted into Park and reached for the door handle, but Arden pressed her shoulder to stop her from getting out.

"No need for both of us to get dirty," he said. As soon as he placed his weight down, he sank far enough into the soggy ground that the muddy water nearly covered the top of his boots. The muck created noticeable suction as he trudged to the front of the car, where he confirmed the driver's side wheel was stuck indeed. "Put it in Reverse," he instructed Rachel, who was sticking her head out the window.

"It is," she confirmed.

"I'm going to rock it a couple times first. On the count of three, apply the gas." Arden bent to place his hands against the front bumper, shoulder width apart, thinking, *This is never an issue with a horse and buggy.* "One… Two…" He could feel the car begin to budge, and he heaved with all his might. "Three!"

Rachel must have pushed the pedal to the floor, because the driver's side wheel gyrated in place, wildly throwing blobs of mud at him before both tires gripped the ground and the car shot backward with such force Arden lost his balance and thumped onto his bottom in the ooze. Fortunately, he was able to halt his backward momentum by bracing his torso with his arms, so he remained in an upright sitting position instead of lying flat in the sludge.

As he wiped dirt from his eyelid with a clear patch

of his sleeve, he saw Rachel charging toward him on foot, waving something white in the air. "Arden, are you okay? I'm so sor—" One of her feet was submerged in mire, and as she extended the other leg forward, it lost traction and slid beneath her. Her knee hit the soft ground first, followed by her elbow on one side and then her palm on the other. By the time she stopped moving, she was lying flat on her belly with her chin in the mud.

Arden scrambled to his feet to help her up, too. "Are you okay?"

"Jah," she said once she was upright. Blinking at the damp, dirty wad she still gripped in her fist, she added, "But I'm afraid these were my only napkins."

The notion that a couple of flimsy paper napkins could have made a difference to them caused Arden to howl with laughter, and Rachel clutched her stomach and joined him. Noticing that the grime on her face made her bright teeth appear even brighter as she laughed, he couldn't think of any woman he knew who would be as good-natured as Rachel was being right now. If her attitude in the face of being drenched with rain and gunk wasn't a demonstration of *demut*, he didn't know what was.

Chapter Six

Once she maneuvered the car into a turn, Rachel offered to take Arden home so he could change his clothes and wash up, but he insisted on continuing to the workshop.

"After the, uh, paint incident, I brought a change of clothing to work. Didn't think I'd need to use them so soon, but…"

Rachel giggled. "But you've never been around me before. I seem to foster all kinds of messy mishaps."

"*Neh*, the paint spill was definitely my fault. But here's a little hint for the next time someone is pushing you out of the mud. You want to apply *light* pressure to the gas pedal."

"How was I supposed to know? I've never been stalled in a swamp before," Rachel countered genially. "Besides, what makes you the expert? You don't drive."

"*Neh*, not anymore. But my running-around period lasted three years, and let's just say there's a lot of snow in Indiana in the winter and flooding in the spring…"

Rachel's mouth fell open. She couldn't imagine staid Arden going through a three-year *rumspringa*. "Wow. My running-around period only lasted four weeks when

I was sixteen. I tried out the *Englisch* lifestyle with my friends, but I honestly wasn't drawn to it."

"But you—" Arden didn't complete his thought.

"I left two years later, *jah*. Despite what people think about me seeking attention or rebelling against my Amish upbringing, that's not why I left. I left because I—" Rachel swallowed the rest of her sentence. She'd said too much.

"You left because…?" Arden twisted toward her in his seat, as if he was truly interested in hearing her answer.

"I left because when my *mamm* was sick, I wished I could do something besides rub her temples and feet with apple cider vinegar or bring her ginger tea." Remembering, Rachel sighed before she clarified, "That doesn't mean I don't value natural remedies, because I do in many instances. But as a young *maedel* watching my *mamm*'s *dokder* and nurses, I developed a curiosity about *Englisch* medicine, and I secretly dreamed of becoming a nurse. But that would have meant leaving the Amish, and after *rumspringa*, I had no desire to go *Englisch*, so I put the idea out of my mind. Then when my *daed* became ill, my fascination with medicine returned and, well, as you know, I eventually became a nurse."

To Rachel's astonishment, instead of Arden pointing out how prideful it was to pursue an *Englisch* education instead of being satisfied with her Amish schooling, he said, "And you became a very *gut* one. *Denki* for helping my *mamm* today."

If Arden didn't know better, he might have suspected it was a tear instead of a trickle of mud dripping down

Rachel's cheek as they pulled into Ivan's driveway. She pushed it aside with the back of her hand and flashed him a smile.

"I'm glad to help your *mamm* any time."

Arden was about to say he hoped his mother wouldn't need help again when he spied movement out of the corner of his eye. An Amish wagon was parked in front of the workshop in the area designated for loading sheds and unloading supplies. Unlike the buggies the Amish in Serenity Ridge used for travel, this type of wagon was pulled by a draft horse instead of a standardbred and had an open seat. Although Arden couldn't see the face of the man who owned the wagon, the steel roof panels piled on the flatbed indicated it belonged to Colin.

"Uh-oh. Look who got caught in the cloudburst."

"I suppose since he's wearing a hat, he figured he didn't need to bring an umbrella," Rachel said, quoting Arden's earlier remark as Colin turned toward them, glaring. On the surface her gibe might have seemed facetious, but beneath it Arden heard a note of fear.

"Hi, Colin. That was quite some del-deluge, eh? Sorry to keep you w-waiting. I see you brought the panels I ordered for the sh-shed roofs." Arden hoped in vain his friendliness would allay Colin's ire.

"I've been sitting here for over an hour. I'm sopping wet and so is my horse. You'd better have a *gut* reason for closing the shop in the middle of the day." As Colin strode in their direction, droplets flew from the brim of his hat. When he removed it to shake it dry, he must have gotten his first full gander at Arden and Rachel, because he abruptly halted and hollered, "Exactly what kind of nonsense have you two been up to this time?"

In the face of confrontation, Arden was usually tongue-tied, but today he struggled to *hold* his tongue. He stood tall with his fingers balled into fists at his sides. "I told you I'd pick up the panels from your shop myself. It was your choice to deliver them and your choice to set out in bad weather. You also chose to *waste time* sitting in the driveway when you could have piled the roofing by the door and left. But then you would have missed the opportunity to scrutinize the business. You can see we're bedraggled and the car is filthy, yet your first inclination isn't to ask about our welfare. It's to cast judgment on me—and on Rachel."

Colin faltered backward two steps before regaining his balance. "If you don't want to tell me where you've been, maybe you'll have to tell Ivan."

Without acknowledging Colin's threat, Arden walked around him to unlock the workshop door and then ambled back to the wagon and began pulling the steel panels from its bed. "Rachel, would you please write a check for Colin for this order?"

"Of course. How much do we owe you?" Rachel sweetly asked her brother.

While she and Colin went inside, Arden finished stacking the metal sheets against the side of the workshop wall. Passing Colin on the way in, he thanked him for the delivery, but Colin didn't reply.

Once inside, Arden headed straight to the rag bin and toweled the grime from his face and hands. Rachel was quiet except to suggest Arden go to the house to change and clean up first, while she minded the shop, and then she took her turn. She came back with two mugs of piping-hot coffee, which Arden found surprisingly refreshing on such a warm day. By then he'd calmed down, but he didn't want to discuss what had happened between Colin and him. He was relieved that once again, Rachel seemed to have an implicit understanding of his need to ruminate in silence. The only thing she told him before they began their separate tasks was that she must have dropped her phone at some point, because she'd discovered it submerged in a puddle on the way to the house.

"Does it still work?"

"*Neh.* I'll stick it in a bowl of dry rice. That sometimes helps."

"You can use the business phone if you need to make any personal calls."

"*Denki*, Arden," she said and when she placed her hand on his arm and held his gaze, he had the feeling she wasn't just talking about the phone.

As she dabbed white paint on the trim of the coop, Rachel tried to sort out her feelings about everything that had happened so far that day. She wished she could talk to Meg, but she didn't want to tie up the business phone. Besides, her roommate might tease her about the jumble of feelings she was experiencing concerning Arden, and Rachel didn't want to joke about it, even in good fun.

She was surprised at herself for confiding in Arden about why she went *Englisch*. Most of the Amish people she'd discussed the subject with had a tendency to *tell* her why she wanted to leave—that was, because of *hochmut* or some other sin—but Arden had truly listened to her explanation, and he didn't seem to judge her for it. *He even said I was a* gut *nurse.* Toby never would have said that—Toby would have criticized her for being confounded by what was triggering Oneita's condition.

As much as she appreciated Arden's kind words, what Rachel found most commendable was how he'd responded to Colin upbraiding him. Without rudeness or rancor, he'd firmly called out Colin's hypocrisy. She was especially touched Arden had made a point to defend Rachel as well as himself against Colin's unfair condemnation.

Colin had appeared so appalled Rachel might have pitied him, had he not threatened to tell Ivan on Arden, as if Arden were a child. How Arden managed to keep his temper Rachel didn't know, but his response inspired her to be civil, too. *How insulting of Colin to insinuate Arden was irresponsible for closing the shop,* she thought. Rachel had witnessed firsthand how much Arden was doing for the business, and this morning she'd seen the burden he was carrying for his mother's health, too. *He's got so much weight on his shoulders.*

Thinking of Arden's shoulders made her pulse skitter, and she set down her paintbrush.

"You dizzy?" Arden called. Had he been watching her?

"A little. I'm going to take my lunch break now, okay?"

"*Jah.* Me, too."

After what they'd been through that morning, it seemed fitting to suggest they eat together, but Rachel resisted the impulse. Her emotions were running high; it was better to put a little distance between Arden and herself until she'd had a good night's sleep. Besides, she intended to spend her break scrubbing the floors. *Ivan's coming home soon. If Colin tells him I've done nothing but made messes, a spotless* haus *will help prove him wrong.*

Arden didn't make it home until nine o'clock on Friday, and after checking with Grace to be sure his sleeping mother hadn't had any more issues with her skin, he took a shower and went to bed. Lying there, he reflected on how Rachel reminded him of Ivan; not only was she finicky about the quality of her painting, but she was discreet like he was, too. She'd promised Arden she wouldn't bring up their altercation with Colin when she visited Ivan that evening.

"We have nothing to hide," she'd said. "But I'd prefer Ivan didn't know about the tension between Colin and me."

"Between Colin and me, too. I shouldn't have responded to him in anger."

"Are you *narrish*? You may have *felt* angry—and justifiably so—but your response wasn't angry. It was truthful and direct. It was very well said, Arden. And you gave him every opportunity to reciprocate with grace."

It was very well said. Arden had never received that compliment before, and he played it over and over in his mind before his thoughts turned to why Rachel had said she'd left the Amish. Despite the rumors, it didn't seem her intention in leaving was to gain knowledge so she could promote herself; she'd left because the *Englisch* gave her an opportunity to serve others in a way she couldn't serve them if she remained in Serenity Ridge. Her decision seemed neither rash nor rebellious—she'd waffled about it for years, primarily because she preferred the Amish lifestyle.

Yet ultimately she did *choose to go* Englisch, Arden reminded himself. *And she* is *going back, so I'd better not get too accustomed to her company, as pleasant as it's turning out to be.*

Although Arden was putting in a full day's work on Saturday, Rachel left the workshop at twelve to pick up Ivan from the hospital, since the staff had confirmed the previous evening he'd be discharged sometime in the afternoon. Arden suggested she take the business phone with her in the event an emergency arose.

"Don't worry," she razzed him. "I learned my lesson yesterday. I'm sticking to the main roads."

"Even the main roads might be flooded. You'll have Ivan with you, and…well, it seems wise to take the phone if case you need it."

Rachel was puzzled by his suggestion, since the Amish relied on the Lord, not on technology, in times of emergency. *I suppose he thinks since I'm not Amish, it's not incongruent for me to carry a phone.* It wasn't, but somehow she didn't want her status as an *Englischer* emphasized.

"Okay, but only because I'm expecting a call from my roommate." Because the business phone didn't have internet access, on Friday Rachel had used it to call Meg to ask her to periodically check her email account for a message from the university. Meg hadn't answered so Rachel left a confidential message along with her email password.

When she arrived at the hospital, an aide was assisting Ivan with his clothing, so Rachel wandered outside and perched on a bench in the sunshine. As a balmy breeze played with the ends of her hair, Rachel watched doctors and nurses entering and exiting the building, their expressions mostly intense. She wondered if that's how she appeared when she arrived for work. There were so many sick people in the world and so many loving family members and friends who worried about them. It often felt overwhelming, and today Rachel was grateful for the slower pace of caring for just one patient, her brother.

When she went back inside, she met one delay after the next in the processing of Ivan's discharge paperwork, even though she'd arrived with his checkbook ready for him to pay the bill. Eventually everything was sorted out, and she brought the car around to pick Ivan up at the entrance. As she and an unfamiliar patient-care assistant helped him into the passenger seat, Ivan tottered, breathless from the brief exertion of standing.

"You sure you're ready to leave? You can stay another night," the assistant jested.

"*Jah*, I'm in *gut* hands. My *schweschder* is a nurse."

Rachel might have been mistaken, but she thought she heard a trace of pride in his voice.

At four o'clock, the customer who ordered the coop came by with several buddies and a truck to transport it home. Afterward, Arden continued working on the shed that was due Monday. Although he'd made enough progress to be confident he'd finish it well before the scheduled pickup time, Arden puttered around the workshop, hoping to greet Ivan. If her brother was as weak as Rachel indicated, he might need help getting into the house.

By six o'clock when they hadn't shown up, Arden began to worry. *What if there is damage to Rachel's car from yesterday and it's acting up now?* His stomach constricted with cramps, and he didn't know if they were from nerves or hunger, but he was determined to stay until Rachel and Ivan arrived.

Unable to focus on work, he took a seat on the bench beneath the peach tree. It had bloomed early this year, and as he leaned against the trunk, inhaling its fragrance and listening to the bees buzzing within the pink blossoms overhead, he quietly prayed until calmness settled over him. Within minutes, Rachel's car wound its way up the driveway. Another soaking rain on Friday afternoon had washed off most of the mud, and her car glinted in the late-day sun.

Arden lifted his hand. He strode to them and opened the front passenger door as Rachel got out on the other side. He was surprised by how loosely Ivan's clothes fit and how much paler he'd become since Arden had seen him last, but his humor was still robust. Grinning at him, Ivan asked, "You didn't think I was coming back, did you?"

"I never doubted it for a second," Arden said, a catch in his voice, because he *had* doubted it. He bent forward so Ivan could sling an arm around his shoulder for support as he rose into a standing position. Arden bolstered Ivan across the lawn at a snail's pace. By the time they got to the porch, Ivan's stamina was depleted.

"Let me rest here in the fresh air," he requested, so Arden lowered him onto the porch swing and took a seat on the bench nearby.

"I made *supp* last night. You'll stay for supper, won't you, Arden?" Rachel asked.

"Supper? I thought Ivan and I would get back to work. There's a shed we need to finish by Monday."

"Oh, sure, now that my *bruder* is back you're going to kick me out of the shop, aren't you?"

"Of course not," Arden objected. "After all, Ivan never brings me *kaffi* and sticky buns in the morning the way you do."

"*Jah*, and I doubt he'd be as forbearing as I was if you ruined *his* paint job."

"*Neh*, probably not, but *he's* never propelled me into a mud puddle like *you* have." Arden recognized they were teasing exaggeratedly for Ivan's benefit, and Ivan seemed to enjoy the entertainment. It felt like a celebration to have him home. That his hospital bill was paid and Arden had nearly met all of their work deadlines added to the festivity.

"It sounds like you two have quite a few stories to tell me," Ivan said. "I can't say *denki* enough to both of you—" He coughed weakly.

"Then don't try," Rachel told him before disappearing into the house for a glass of water.

"She's right. Or I'll have to try to figure out a way to say *denki* for all the times you've helped me. And we both know how *gut* I am with words." Usually Arden didn't acknowledge his speaking difficulties, even in jest, but this evening he felt less self-conscious than ever before. Rachel reappeared with the water for Ivan and then went back into the house, telling them supper would be ready in a few minutes.

"How is your *mamm*?" Ivan questioned.

"She was struggling for a while. She experienced some new symptoms, which are already improving, thanks to your *schweschder*."

"That's *gut*." Ivan closed his eyes and smiled as a breeze passed over the lawn, carrying the scent of peach blossoms and new grass.

They sat in comfortable silence until Rachel announced supper was ready. She stepped outside to steady the swing so Arden could assist her brother out of it. He used his shoulder to truss Ivan beneath one arm while Rachel did the same on the opposite side. The three of them were about to angle toward the door when Ivan said softly, "Well, look at that. I think my first visitor has arrived."

Perplexed that someone could have come up the driveway without her hearing them and nervous it might have been Colin, Rachel followed the direction of Ivan's eyes. In the gloaming she could just make out a form on the far periphery of the front lawn. A bear? An enormous deer?

"A moose!" Arden uttered in a hushed tone, and the great animal swung its head in their direction. For nearly a full minute, it kept utterly still before it turned and lumbered into the woods bordering the property.

"That was amazing. I've never seen a moose the whole time I've lived here," Ivan said.

"Me, neither," Rachel said. "I mean, when I lived here before. I wish my phone worked. I would have liked to take a photo to show to Meg. Maybe it'll come back."

"If he does, it's *schmaert* to steer clear of him," Arden said. "He might look docile, but moose are unpredictable. His antlers haven't fully *kumme* in this year, but if he charged, he could kick or trample a person to death."

After the trio squeezed through the door, Ivan said,

"It must have been all the excitement, but I'm too bushed to eat. Arden, could you help me out? I'd like to go to bed, but I feel as unwieldy as that moose."

While Arden was assisting her brother in the bedroom down the hall, Rachel filled two bowls with soup and placed a loaf of bread on the table and then poured the milk. When Arden reentered the room and seated himself opposite her, she felt strangely shy to be eating alone with him, even though they worked together side by side every day.

"I'll say grace," she offered, bowing her head. "Lord, *denki* for healing Ivan and bringing him home. And *denki* for bringing me home at this time, too." Her voice quavered, so she paused a moment. "Please continue to heal Arden's *mamm* and help her to get the care she needs. Soften my heart toward Colin and soften his heart to me and both of our hearts to You. Please strengthen us with this food, especially Arden, who needs endurance as he continues to labor so diligently in the workshop during Ivan's recovery. Amen." Rachel furtively dabbed a tear away before lifting her head.

Arden's celestial-blue eyes searched hers. "Are you okay?" he asked. She was embarrassed he'd caught her tearing up until he added, "Your hand is bleeding."

"Bleeding? Where?" She turned her hands palm up and then over again.

He leaned across the table and gently twisted her hand to indicate the space between her ring and middle fingers. "There."

Rachel's breath hitched. Instead of taking her hand from his to get a better look, she leaned forward to see the red stain. Although she instantly recognized what it was, she didn't want to say. Not yet, not if saying it meant he withdrew his touch.

"See it?" Arden asked.

"It's paint, from the coop," she replied, embarrassed that she'd washed her hands countless times but clearly hadn't done a good enough job. To her surprise, he allowed her fingers to linger in his.

"Oh. I guess it's a *gut* thing *I'm* not the one taking care of Ivan, since I can't even tell the difference between blood and paint," Arden joked, giving her hand a little squeeze. Only then did he release it, sliding his arm back across the table and picking up his spoon.

The soup scalded Arden's tongue and gave him something to distract him from the topsy-turvy way he was feeling. As he chugged down half a glass of milk, Rachel remarked how tired Ivan still seemed.

"*Jah*, he practically dozed off midsentence in his room."

"I'll have to wake him soon for his medication. And to check for a fever. They said to watch for that. A relapse of pneumonia can be even worse than the initial bout."

"You're going to need endurance, too."

"What?"

"You prayed I'd have endurance. You're going to need it, too," Arden explained. "There were a lot of nurses in the hospital, but here you're on your own."

"Don't you think I'm qualified to take care of him by myself?"

That wasn't what he'd meant at all. Arden was surprised by the plea for reassurance in Rachel's question; usually she seemed so confident. "I can't think of anyone better qualified to take care of him. But he's got a long road to recovery ahead, and you're going to need help so you don't wear yourself out."

"I told Hadassah I'd *wilkom* her help, but I don't think I can count on her. Joyce and Albert won't return from Canada for a couple more weeks, according to Ivan."

"In addition to Grace, there are others in the community who will be *hallich* to help."

"I don't know about that. I'm worried they'll stay away because of my presence. Maybe Ivan would have been better off without me here. Maybe my coming here was a mistake."

"*Neh.* It wasn't a mistake." Upon seeing the fragile vulnerability in Rachel's eyes, Arden's heart ballooned with compassion. "Trust me, the community will *kumme* to help."

"In that case, I'd better keep dessert and tea on hand," Rachel said, smiling once again.

"Does that mean we can't have a slice of that pie over there?"

"Of course it doesn't. And since Ivan has no appetite, you and I might as well have large pieces."

Supping with Rachel after a hard day's work, encouraging her and discussing Ivan's care as if he were…not a child, but *like* a child, felt…well, it felt like how Arden always imagined it would feel if he had a family of his own. Which was probably why, half an hour later as he directed his horse toward home, Arden's stomach was full, but he couldn't shake the aching emptiness he felt inside.

Having checked on Ivan throughout the night, Rachel was wearier in the morning than she'd been when she went to bed. Since it was an off Sunday, she suggested she and Ivan hold their own worship services together. She was delighted when he told her he'd kept their father's old Bible in a drawer upstairs. Rachel read aloud from it in German. Although she hadn't practiced the language in years, the words returned to her as readily as the vistas of Serenity Ridge, so familiar and beautiful she wondered how she'd gone so long without them.

When she finished reading, she prepared a light lunch and then Ivan needed to sleep again, so Rachel helped him into the bedroom and then tiptoed away, leaving the door slightly ajar so she could hear if he summoned her. She was drying their dishes when a buggy approached; it was Arden's.

"Grace wanted me to deliver these whoopie pies. She thinks they'll whet Ivan's appetite for home-cooked food again." He handed her a square plastic container with a note taped on top of it, reading:

> Rachel,
> *Mamm* and I are expecting visitors this afternoon or I would have *kumme* to see you and Ivan myself. We are praying for you both.
> Grace

"Oh, that's so thoughtful. These *are* Ivan's favorite, but it feels like there are plenty in here. Would you like one?" After experiencing such an enjoyable time with Arden at supper the previous night, Rachel didn't hesitate to invite him to share dessert this afternoon.

"*Jah*, please. When I asked if I could have one at home, Grace refused. Apparently, whoopie pies are only for people with pneu-pneumon-pneumonia," Arden complained as he lowered himself onto the bench. "Or for p-people taking care of p-people with pneumonia."

"*Neh*, they're also for people visiting people taking care of people with pneumonia," Rachel said with a giggle.

A few minutes later as they were indulging in the treats and tea, another buggy pulled into the driveway. Upon seeing it was Hadassah, Rachel nearly fell off the porch swing. *Maybe she's had a change of heart!*

Smiling, Rachel waved as Arden hurried to help her sister-in-law from the buggy. Two of the children scrambled down in front of her. Hadassah's pregnant belly seemed to have grown impossibly larger in the past few days.

Aware questions about her sister-in-law's health would be unwelcome, Rachel greeted her by saying, "Hello, Hadassah. It's so nice to see you." Then she bent to speak to the children. "Hello again, Thomas. And you must be Sarah. Your *onkel* Ivan wrote to me about you. I'm your *ant* Rachel."

Without responding, Thomas took off to chase a squirrel across the yard, but to Rachel's amazement, Sarah said, "Hello, *Ant* Rachel," and then joined her brother. Rachel couldn't help but notice the girl looked more like Rachel than like Hadassah—with one unfortunate difference; Sarah's nose was running. In fact, Thomas had a runny nose, too. The nurse in Rachel wondered how long they'd been ill.

Without acknowledging Rachel's greeting, Hadassah said, "The *kinner* want to see their *onkel*. Is he inside?"

"*Jah*, but he's sleeping."

"That's okay. We've *kumme* all this way. Thomas and Sarah can play in the yard until he wakes. I'll sit beneath the peach tree." She began plodding across the sodden ground.

"You're *wilkom* to join us on the porch, Hadassah," Rachel called after her. "But I'm afraid today isn't a *gut* day for you and the *kinner* to visit Ivan. It seems Sarah and Thomas have colds, and we don't want to jeopardize Ivan's recovery."

Hadassah slowly pivoted toward the house, her features contorted into a scowl. Breathing heavily, she approached the porch and shook her pointer finger at Rachel. "It's one thing for you to believe you're superior to the Amish. But how can you can be so puffed up as to think you know more about health care than the *Englisch*? Not one of those nurses in the hospital ever prohibited me from seeing Ivan, and I'm not going to let you stop me, either!"

As peeved as Hadassah's remarks made her, Rachel had enough experience dealing with patients' families to respond calmly. "If the nurses in the hospital saw Sarah and Thomas today, they wouldn't allow them to visit Ivan, either. He simply can't be exposed to any infections right now. Even a common cold could wreak havoc on his immune system, because it's already severely compromised."

"My *kinner* do *not* have colds. They have allergies."

"*Neh*, they have colds. Their mucus is not running clear—"

"*Absatz!* I don't want to hear you describe such a thing to me. Even if you're right—which you are *not*—I do not have a cold and *I'm* going to see Ivan." Her face and neck were crimson as she set one foot on the bottom stair.

"You may not have a cold yet, but you've been in

close contact with least two *kinner* who do." Rachel planted herself in front of the doorway. "We must guard Ivan's health. And I hope you'll guard your own health, too, because you don't want to *kumme* down with something this late in your pregnancy. I appreciate what an effort it was for you to *kumme* here, and I'd *wilkom* your company here on the porch. How about if I bring you and the *kinner* some refreshments?"

Without answering her, Hadassah questioned Arden, "Do you hear how she's speaking to me?"

"I think Rachel's right, Hadassah," Arden replied. "Please don't get so worked up about it, though. As soon as the *kinner* are over their colds, you can visit."

"Pah!" Hadassah puffed. She leaned on her knee with one hand and used the other to point at Arden this time. "Colin warned me about you two. I believed what he said about Rachel, but I didn't want to believe him about you, Arden. You'd better be careful cozying up to an *Englischer*. It wouldn't sit right with the bishop."

As she trudged away, Arden scurried down the porch steps, offering, "Let me help you into the buggy, Hadassah," but she batted at his hand. Instead she leaned on the shoulders of her children, who teetered beneath her weight.

So much for the community helping me, Rachel lamented to herself. *I'll be fortunate if I'm not ousted from Serenity Ridge altogether once Hadassah and Colin are done wagging their chins about me.*

Chapter Seven

After Hadassah's buggy rolled down the driveway, Arden went to bid Rachel goodbye, but she'd gone into the house, undoubtedly to tend to Ivan.

On his way home, he wondered, *Why wouldn't Colin accompany his wife to his* bruder*'s* haus *when she obviously has a difficult time with mobility? What could possibly be more important than seeing to Hadassah's comfort and safety?* Deep down, Arden suspected Colin was deliberately slighting Rachel—at his wife's expense—as a demonstration of his anger. He could only imagine how much angrier Colin would be once Hadassah told him Rachel had turned her away and Arden had defended Rachel's decision.

Their behavior is unfair. I'm *the one who should go to the bishop about* them, Arden thought. *I'd be perfectly justified.* But he wouldn't do that, because while the Bible said God required His people to "do justly," it also instructed them to love mercy. Besides, Arden was confident he'd done nothing wrong, so he wasn't overly concerned about what Colin or Hadassah might say if they actually did report him to the bishop. Still, Arden decided, for Ivan's sake, he ought to tread carefully. For Rachel's sake, too. There was already enough tension between the Blank family members; he didn't want to add to it by appearing to side with Rachel. Hadassah and Colin could make her time in Serenity Ridge very unpleasant, and Arden didn't want her being squeezed out before Ivan was better. The very fact that Hadassah had brought sick children to visit their uncle showed just how much Ivan needed someone like Rachel there, advocating for his health. *The less time I spend with her outside the workshop, the better it will be for everyone*, Arden concluded.

When he arrived home, Arden was dismayed to find Ike and Eva Renno, whose buggy he'd passed on the road as he set out to deliver the whoopie pies, were seated in the double wooden glider on the porch. Although Arden liked Ike and Eva was a nice enough person, she was as chatty as Arden was reserved, and his head throbbed whenever he spent more than fifteen minutes in her presence.

"*Mamm* went inside to nap. She said she couldn't think of a better way for any *mamm* to celebrate Mother's Day," Grace informed him when he hopped up the steps. Because Mother's Day fell on the Sabbath, the Amish in Serenity Ridge didn't make a fuss over it, although Arden and Grace had gifted their mother with a subscription to her favorite publication, *The Connection*, which was published out of Indiana and included articles written by Amish people throughout the country. "I made iced tea. *Kumme* join our discussion."

"I've, uh, already had tea," Arden hedged.

"Oh, were you out visiting someone special?" Eva questioned.

Arden could have kicked himself for letting that slip. "On second thought, I'm kind of hot. I would like a glass, please."

"Were you visiting someone special?" Eva repeated.

"I, uh, stopped by Ivan's *haus*."

"Ivan's *haus*? I heard his *Englisch schweschder* is staying there."

I guess the cat's out of the bag now. Holding out his hand to take the glass from his sister, Arden replied noncommittally, "*Jah*, that's correct."

"Sit down," Grace insisted and waited for Arden to take a seat before giving him the iced tea. "How was Ivan?"

"He was asleep again, so I didn't get to speak to him. Rachel said he had a restless night—he was coughing a lot."

"Oh, the poor dear. I have a tried-and-true honey-cider cough remedy I could bring him, don't I, Ike? Remember when I gave it to you last October when you were sick with bronchitis?" Eva didn't wait for her husband to reply before resuming her earlier train of thought. "Maybe I shouldn't bother bringing it to Ivan, though. Hadassah said the *Englisch schweschder* has taken control of his health—in addition to his *haus* and his business, but I don't have to tell *you* that, do I, Arden?—so I don't know if my gesture would be *wilkom*."

Arden felt the hair on the back of his neck stand on end, and he reminded himself it was better to say nothing; that way, his comments couldn't be misinterpreted.

Grace, however, piped up, "I'm sure Rachel would appreciate an act of kindness from someone in our community. She might be pleased to receive visitors, too, provided they don't overstay their *wilkom*."

There was no mistaking the implication in Grace's remark, but it seemed lost on Eva. "To be frank, I don't know if I want to visit Ivan while the *schweschder* is there. Hadassah said she's been flaunting her *Englisch* ways in front of her *familye*. Showing up at Hadassah's *haus* uninvited in her car, or wearing inappropriate hairstyles and clothing in front of her *dochdere*, that kind of thing. I don't want her pushing her lifestyle on *me* like that."

Arden could no longer censor himself. "I've been w-working with Rachel at the shop, and she never w-wears or does anything in-in-inappropriate. *Jah*, she's *Englisch*, but she's also very m-modest."

Eva raised an eyebrow. "You find her becoming, don't you?"

How could she twist my words like that? No matter how he replied, Arden figured he'd incriminate himself, so he refused to say another word. Grace, on the other hand, let loose.

"*Jah*, Rachel is very fetching, and she's very *schmaert*, too. More importantly, she's extremely helpful," she said. "She helped *Mamm* when she was experiencing new lupus symptoms, and she told us about as many alternative forms of treatment as *Englisch* ones. So if that's your concern about sharing your remedy, you have nothing to worry about. She demonstrates every bit as much respect toward the Amish as the Amish demonstrate toward her."

Although Arden wholeheartedly agreed with Grace's characterization of Rachel, he was concerned if her comments got back to Hadassah, they'd make things worse. Fortunately, once again his sister's words seemed to go right over Eva's head; she'd turned her attention to swatting at a bee.

"Ike! It's going to sting me," she whined, flapping her hands about her ears. Her husband jumped to his feet and fanned his hat through the air.

Arden took advantage of their alarm to change the subject. "Guess what I saw yesterday? A moose!"

Eva immediately stopped flailing to inform everyone moose had been spotted in the deacon's yard, on the Christmas tree farm and at the lake, as well. Arden asked enough questions to keep her talking on the subject for half an hour until another bee chased her from her chair and her husband suggested they'd better be on their way.

As she lay in bed on Sunday evening, Rachel reflected on Hadassah's earlier remarks. She vacillated between feeling utterly incensed and being racked with guilt. On one hand, her sister-in-law had been completely out of line to speak to her as she did. Couldn't Hadassah see Rachel's refusal to allow her to visit Ivan wasn't personal? She was only looking out for her brother's best interests.

Yet, having witnessed how labored Hadassah's breathing was and having watched her struggling to walk even a short distance, Rachel was worried about her sister-in-law's health, too. It wasn't good for her to get so upset. As necessary as it was to keep Hadassah from seeing Ivan, Rachel regretted having caused her distress, especially when she belatedly realized today was Mother's Day. Knowing Colin, Rachel doubted he'd given Hadassah a card or even verbally acknowledged her devotion to their children, so she was probably in need of encouragement.

Even so, why should I *be the one lying here feeling sorry for upsetting* her? *I doubt she feels guilty for hurting my feelings by announcing my own* bruder *warned her about me.* Actually, Hadassah had said Colin had warned her about *them*—meaning both Rachel *and* Arden. Rachel didn't know exactly what that meant, but she had an inkling. And if Colin and Hadassah really did go to the bishop with their grievances, who would the bishop be more likely to believe—an *Englischer* who abandoned her community or an Amish couple who'd lived in Serenity Ridge since they were *kinner*? Rachel didn't want to find out. Nor did she want to put Arden in the position of having to defend himself.

My main objective is to help Ivan with his business and his recovery. I'm only here temporarily, she reminded herself. Long after she returned to Boston, the others would still be working and living in Serenity Ridge. It was important to Rachel that their long-term relationships with each other didn't suffer because of her short-term presence among them now. For that reason, she decided she'd try to do whatever she could to prevent and ease any discord between them. *I should distance myself from Arden whenever possible, too, so no one else can accuse him of "cozying up to an Englischer."*

Yet the idea of giving up her budding friendship with Arden made her so resentful Rachel rolled out of bed and knelt beside it in prayer. *Dear* Gott, *I want You to use me to reflect Your love, but I don't feel very loving at the moment. Please change my heart and give me strength.* Upon hearing Ivan's coughing downstairs, she added, *And please give Ivan strength, too.*

But the next morning, Rachel's brother seemed even weaker than he'd been on Sunday, and despite his objections, she refused to go to the shop to work. Instead, she decided she'd gather whatever paperwork she needed and bring it back to the house, where she'd also field customer calls while keeping an eye on Ivan. When she scurried to the workshop to tell Arden her plan, he barely glanced up from the tiny structure he was building.

"What's that, a dollhouse to go inside Mrs. McGregor's playhouse?" she joshed.

"It's a doghouse," he replied flatly and then resumed hammering.

Rachel squinted at him, wondering if he'd simply gotten up on the wrong side of the bed or if something else had gone awry. Was it possible Colin and Hadassah had already filled the bishop's ear with their tales about him and her? "Is everything all right?"

"*Jah*, just busy," he mumbled and drove another nail into a joist. Rachel waited for him to stop hammering.

"Then you won't like what I have to tell you. I have to work up at the *haus* today because I don't want to leave Ivan alone. I'm afraid of what might happen if he gets out of bed by himself. His legs are still a bit rickety. One *gut* spring breeze and he'd collapse like a *haus* of cards." Rachel tittered nervously.

"There's no need for you to be here today anyway, so that's fine."

Keeping my distance from him isn't going to be such a loss after all, Rachel thought as she collected what she needed from the desk and returned to the house.

But by the end of the day, she almost would have preferred Arden's grouchy company to no company at all, since Ivan slept most of the day. Although she was aware his recovery would be slow, Rachel fretted over her brother's condition, second-guessing whether he'd been released from the hospital too soon. On Tuesday morning, however, he awoke looking bright-eyed and declaring how hungry he was. She settled him into a chair at the kitchen table and poured them each a cup of coffee.

"I'll make *oier* and *pannekuche*," she offered, retrieving eggs from the fridge and a mixing bowl from the cupboard.

Ivan said something that sounded like, "Don brfr," and she twirled around to catch him with a mouthful of the whoopie pie he must have taken from the container on the table. He swallowed before repeating, "Don't bother. I'll just have one of these." When he smiled at her, his teeth were comically blackened from the dark cake, and she laughed so hard she dropped into a chair opposite him.

"What's so funny?" he asked, so she took a whoopie pie for herself, bit into it and then grinned back at him. They both cracked up until she begged him to stop because she was afraid he'd lose his breath and wind up back in the hospital.

"Nonsense," he said. "I haven't felt this *gut* in weeks."

Circling the table, Rachel wrapped her arms around his scrawny shoulders and kissed the top of his head. "Neither have I."

"You ought to go back to the workshop," he told her when she released him.

"*Neh*. Maybe tomorrow, if you keep improving."

"Arden probably needs your help today more than I do."

Rachel hesitated. Arden had likely finished the doghouse by now, and it would need to be painted. "Let's compromise. At lunchtime, I'll send Arden here to visit you during his break, and I'll go get a few things done in the shop."

When she trekked to the workshop shortly before one o'clock, Rachel spotted Arden in the driveway talking to an *Englischer* she assumed was a customer, so she went inside and set the folders she'd been carrying on the desk. The business phone buzzed, and as she reached for it, she accidentally knocked a file to the floor, scattering invoices everywhere.

"Hi, Rach. It's me, Meg. I know this is your business phone, but—"

Her heart leaped to her throat. "Did I get into the MSN program?"

"No," Meg said. "I mean, that's not why I'm calling. I checked your email, but there wasn't any notice yet. I'm sorry to get your hopes up. It was just that your message was so cryptic the other day I wanted to be sure you're okay."

"Oh." Rachel sighed. "Yeah, I, well… Friday was a long day, but everything is fine now. Ivan's home now."

"Hey, that's great! That means *you'll* be home soon, too. Unless you decide to stay."

"How many times do I have to tell you, I am *not* staying here," Rachel contended. *And I might be returning sooner rather than later if Hadassah has her way.*

"Uh-oh. Does that mean Mr. Morose hasn't gotten any nicer to you since you've been in Serenity Ridge?"

"What? Do you mean Toby?" Distracted by picking

up the invoices, Rachel didn't have the foggiest notion why her roommate would have thought she'd been in touch with Toby.

"No, not Dr. Deceiver. I was referring to Amish Arden. You know, Mr. Morose. The kind of thoughtless, insensitive man you're supposedly trying to avoid."

"Oh, him. Well, like I've said, he isn't always *that* dull. I definitely wouldn't put him in the same category as Toby," Rachel said. She knew Meg's nicknames were her impish way of sticking up for Rachel, but she was relieved she hadn't shared her ambivalence about Arden with her roommate. It wasn't something she wanted to make light of. "So, anything new happening with you?"

"Aside from the landlord finally fixing the washing machine? Nope, not a thing."

"I am so envious," Rachel joked. "Nothing that exciting has happened here, although we did see a moose last evening…"

After a few minutes of chitchat, Meg promised to let Rachel know as soon as she got an email from the university and then hung up. As Rachel stood to stack the mess of papers she'd gathered on the desk, she noticed Arden in the doorway.

"Hi, Arden. I've *kumme* to switch places with you. How about if I stay here and paint the doghouse while you take your lunch break at the *haus*, where you can keep an eye on Ivan? He's been guarding the whoopie pies, but if you arm wrestle him for one, I'm sure you'd win," she jested.

"*Neh*. I got waylaid by another project, so I haven't completed the doghouse yet. I'm not taking a lunch break. So there's no sense in you hanging around here this afternoon."

His reply was so curt and his tone so dismissive that Rachel stalked off thinking, *As if I'd want to be around you anyway,* Mr. Morose!

Arden sawed through a two-by-six, letting the end segment clatter to the floor before stopping to take a swig of cold water. It quenched his thirst but not his fuming. He'd been mad ever since he overheard Rachel talking on the phone. It wasn't as if he'd intended to listen in on her conversation, but now that he'd overheard it, her words echoed ruthlessly in his mind.

"He isn't always *that* dumb," she'd said. Or had she used the word *dull*? It hardly mattered; they meant the same thing—she'd been calling someone stupid. Maybe it was self-centered of Arden to suspect *he* was the one she'd been referring to, but who else could she have meant? Her brothers were the only other men she'd crossed paths with in Serenity Ridge, and she regarded Ivan too highly to speak about him that way. As for Colin, he was cantankerous, maybe even cruel, but Arden doubted Rachel considered him dumb—not even compared to Toby, who apparently was so intelligent he was in a class all by himself. That left Arden.

He felt humiliated. He felt infuriated. And, ironically, he felt extraordinarily stupid—not because of his speaking and reading difficulties, but because he'd sincerely believed Rachel respected him. Come to find out she was looking down her nose at him, maybe even at the entire Amish community. *I guess Colin and Hadassah were right about her after all.* Her phone conversation had made it clear not only how she felt about Arden but about being in Serenity Ridge, where apparently nothing exciting happened. *Sorry we don't live up to your standards for entertainment,* he imagined saying to her. *If you're so bored, why don't you hire a visiting nurse to take care of Ivan so you can go back to the* Englisch *lifestyle you claimed you were never drawn to in the first place?*

Arden's foul mood followed him throughout the afternoon, but at least he channeled his orneriness into constructing the small, simple garden shed that was due the following morning. It was a quick project that required no painting, but without Rachel on-site to remind him of the deadline, he'd forgotten about it. Unfortunately, that meant he'd have to stay late to complete the doghouse that was due on Thursday, which would have to be painted tomorrow. He was so engrossed in his work he didn't notice anyone had entered the workshop until Grace appeared at his side.

"What's wrong—"

"Don't worry, *Mamm*'s fine. She insisted I bring supper to Rachel and Ivan. And to you, too. She thought we'd enjoy sharing a meal together."

I'm sure she did. "That's a nice gesture, but I'm too busy to stop for supper."

"But you've got to eat."

"Eating can wait. My deadline can't."

"You don't have to stay long, but surely you can spare the time to gobble down a plate of *yumsetta,*" Grace argued. "C'mon, Arden. If you don't join us, it will look like…you know."

"Like you're here specifically to see Ivan because you like him?" Although he had never mentioned it before, Arden had his suspicions about how his sister felt about Ivan. The color rising in her cheeks now indicated he'd been right.

"*Neh*, it will look like you're being rude. Which you *are*, in more ways than one!" Grace retorted. Arden hadn't meant to insult her; he'd just wanted her to back off about eating supper at the house.

"Ivan knows how much work I have to do. He'll understand why I can't stop."

"*Jah*, but what about Rachel? Have you considered how she might feel if you don't join us for a meal? She might think it's because she's *Englisch*."

"Rachel *is Englisch*, and I have no obligation to socialize with her. My only obligation is to *work* with her."

"Eh-hem." From the doorway, Rachel cleared her throat. "I, um, was coming to ask whether you prefer water or *millich* with your meal."

"*Millich*, please," Grace answered. "Arden can't eat with us tonight—he's got to keep working."

"I understand." Rachel looked squarely at him. Arden couldn't read her expression, but after she and Grace left, he wondered, *Did she hear what I said about not being obligated to socialize with her?* Then he shrugged it off, reasoning, *Now she knows what it's like to overhear someone express how they* really *feel about you.*

But the truth was, Arden *didn't* really feel about Rachel the way his comment might have made it sound, even if *she* thought *he* was dumb. Which he had to admit was kind of presumptuous—maybe even egotistical—of him to believe, since he couldn't be certain she'd been talking about him on the phone. The more time that passed, the hungrier he became, and the more he wished he had joined the others for supper. *Maybe if I hurry I can finish this up and get to the* haus *before Grace leaves. If I'm fortunate, I can at least get a piece of dessert.*

By the time he'd completed his work on the doghouse, it was after seven, so he didn't bother to put his tools away before locking up for the night. As he crossed the driveway, he spotted Ivan and Grace rocking on the porch swing, and he wondered if they'd already had dessert or if Rachel would serve it to them there. But from this vantage point, he could see the backyard, too, and he noticed Rachel was taking in the laundry—an indication her hosting duties had ended.

The clothesline was a bit too high; she had to stand on tiptoes to grasp it and then tug it down while she unclipped the pins. As Arden quickened his pace so he could give her a hand, he spied something looming near the back perimeter of the property. At first he thought it was a shadow or the dusk was playing tricks on his eyes, but then the creature slogged several steps in Rachel's direction. *The moose!* Arden's heart battered his ribs. Although the animal's eyesight likely wasn't good enough for it to see Rachel behind the linens, its hearing and sense of smell were excellent, and it seemed to home in on her. By contrast, Rachel was completely oblivious to the danger lurking on the other side of the sheet hanging in front of her.

Aware a loud noise could frighten the moose, Arden crept closer and said, "Rachel, *absatz*," just loud enough for her to hear. She swiveled her head sideways to look at him, an annoyed expression on her face as she continued unpinning the sheet. "Do. Not. Move," he commanded gruffly, terrified she'd flounce off rather than speak to him. "There's a moose coming toward you."

His tone must have convinced her he was gravely serious, because Rachel froze with her arms stretched above her head, her spine straight. She locked her gaze on him, and her face went whiter than the sheet she'd was unfastening. "Arden, help me," she whimpered. Then, "Please help me, Lord. Please, *Gott*, make it go away."

Arden tried to reassure her from where he'd sought protection beside a maple tree some ten yards away. The tree wasn't especially wide, but he knew it was vital to keep something sturdy in between him and the moose at all times. "It stopped walking, but it's looking your way. You must do exactly what I tell you to do. If I say run, you need to sprint over here to me, behind this tree as fast as you can."

"Now?"

"Neh!" Arden exclaimed, and the moose lowered its head and flattened its ears, both signs of aggression. "Don't run unless I tell you to."

"Please, Arden, please," she pleaded, as if he held any authority over the large bull. "It's getting closer. I can hear it making a clicking sound."

"Rachel, listen to me. I want you to back away very, very slowly." She immediately let go of the clothesline and sheet and inched away as the moose flattened its ears—not a good sign. Arden's back and leg muscles were so tense they burned. Little by little Rachel was putting distance between herself and the moose, but she was still out in the open. She couldn't outrun the animal if it charged; she'd never make it around the house or even to the maple tree.

Arden considered his options. If he waved and yelled, there was a chance the moose might scram, but it seemed more likely he'd incite the beast to charge. So he did the only thing he could count on to be effective: *Please, Gott, get that animal out of here*, he prayed.

"Arden, what are you looking for over there?" Grace questioned loudly as she came traipsing around the house toward the backyard.

"Shh." Arden gestured for Grace to stop just as the dangling sheet billowed in the breeze. At that the moose thundered forward. "Run!" Arden shouted, but instead Rachel collapsed right where she stood. Arden started to race toward her when he noticed the moose had come to an abrupt standstill a few yards in front of the clothesline, so he halted, too. The bull's first charge was a bluff. Would it leave or would it charge a second time for real?

"Don't move," he growled at Grace, who'd also stopped dead in her tracks. He waited as the moose stared at the sheet. Was that what it was after all along? One, maybe two agonizing minutes passed before the animal slowly raised its head again and galumphed from the yard.

Grace and Arden both sprinted toward Rachel. He reached her first, and she was already rousing, or trying to. He rolled her from her side onto her back and directed Grace to elevate Rachel's feet twelve inches above her heart. Then he bent to put his ear by her mouth so he could hear her raspy voice.

"Did the moose knock me down?"

"*Neh.* He didn't have to. You fell down on your own."

"Where did everyone go?" Ivan asked, stumbling toward them in the twilight.

"Wait right there!" Grace ordered. "We don't need a second Blank passing out tonight." She gently set Rachel's feet down and ran to Ivan's side, saying, "I'll take him inside."

When Rachel lifted her head and propped herself up

on her elbows, Arden warned, "You shouldn't get up too quickly. You might get dizzy."

"Who's the nurse here, you or me?" she asked, sitting all the way up.

"I might not be as *schmaert* as you are, but I'm definitely stronger," Arden replied. He slid an arm beneath her knees and wrapped his other one around her torso. In one swift motion, he stood upright and pulled her closer to his trembling heart.

Arden's gesture was so unexpected and his embrace so gentle Rachel felt as if she might faint a second time. As he carried her toward the house, she exhaled, allowing herself to go limp against his chest. She was so accustomed to being a nurse—to caring for others—she didn't realize how soothing it was to have someone coddle *her*, and she closed her eyes to bask in the feeling.

"You okay?" Arden's breath warmed Rachel's face.

"Jah." She peered up at him. *"Denki* for rescuing me. If you hadn't warned me the moose was there or talked me through the situation, who knows what might have happened."

"I hardly *rescued* you. That was *Gott*'s doing."

"True, but *Gott* allowed you to be in the right place at the right time, so He could use you for my *gut*."

They reached the house, and Arden climbed the porch stairs and opened the screen door one-handed, not setting her down until they'd reached the living room, where Grace was coaxing Ivan to take another sip of water.

"Rachel!" Ivan exclaimed. "Grace told me what happened. Praise the Lord you're all right."

"Praise the Lord you're all right, too," Rachel echoed.

Arden still had his arm looped around her waist, and he assisted her to the sofa so she could sit next to her brother. Once seated, she patted Ivan's hand. "You hardly have enough strength to walk from the bedroom to the living room, much less hike through the yard. What would you have done if the moose had charged *you*?"

"That would depend."

"On what?"

"On how much money I had," Ivan deadpanned.

"Voll schpass." Everyone laughed until Rachel clapped her hand over her mouth, realizing she needed to pick up a prescription. The pharmacy at the superstore was open until ten, and the druggist had said they'd have the medication ready, since Ivan needed to take it that night before bed.

"I don't think you should drive," Arden protested. "Not so soon after fainting."

"I'll be fi—"

"Neh, she definitely shouldn't drive." Grace agreed with her brother for once. "You ought to take her in the buggy, Arden. I'll stay with Ivan."

"Neh. It will take too long. Your *mamm* will be worried."

"Our *mamm* will be asleep," Grace countered. "She told me she was going to bed early and we shouldn't hurry home if we're having *schpass*, especially Arden. She's always pestering him to be more social."

Rachel got the feeling *Grace* was the one who was in no hurry to return home; clearly she desired to spend more time talking with Ivan alone on the porch. While Rachel empathized, she could tell by Arden's lack of response how hesitant he was to bring her to the pharmacy. All of a sudden, she remembered his words from earlier that day: "Rachel *is Englisch* and I have no obligation to socialize with her." In her hysteria over the moose, she'd forgotten about that and how hurt and disappointed she'd felt. Granted, it was a small offense compared to the enormity of saving her life, so she couldn't hold a grudge. Neither could she impose on Arden to spend more time with her than he wanted to— especially since she'd already committed to distancing herself from *him*.

"*Neh*, that's okay. I'll be fine driving," Rachel said. Then to show she held no expectation of him, she added, "Arden's not obligated to take me."

"I know I'm not obligated," Arden said, his tone as assertive as when he'd instructed Rachel not to move as the moose was eyeing her. "But I'd *like* to take you, if you'll let me."

Concerned he may have felt put on the spot, Rachel questioned, "Are you sure you don't mind?"

Arden didn't reply—he was already on his way outside to hitch up his horse and buggy.

Chapter Eight

Arden's ears were scorching; Rachel had *definitely* heard what he'd said to Grace in the workshop. As he adjusted the leather straps on the horse's harness, he wondered how he was going to explain why he felt it was necessary to avoid her outside the workshop. The horse whinnied, and Arden glanced around the driveway to make sure the moose hadn't returned. A shiver prickled his spine. *Rachel could have died tonight*, he thought. Suddenly, he felt resentful of Colin and Hadassah's pettiness. If they didn't value the opportunity to have a relationship with Rachel, that was their choice, but he wasn't going to let their opinion—their self-righteousness and spite—ruin *his* friendship with her.

So, after he assisted Rachel into the buggy but before he directed the horse to walk on, he turned to her and said, "I kn-know you overheard what I told Grace in the w-work-sh-shop about not being o-obligated to s-socialize with you. I only said that because I—I—I felt bad Colin and Hadassah were so upset, and I thought by not sp-spending time with you except at work, maybe it would help e-e-ease the ten-tension." It had been a while since Arden's speech had been that choppy in Rachel's presence, and a bead of sweat dribbled down his neck.

She nodded thoughtfully. "I understand. I actually decided something similar about limiting the time I spend with you. Not just for Ivan's sake, either—I don't want you to get a bad reputation if you hang out with me socially. You know, guilt by association."

Arden shrugged. "Neither of us is guilty of any wrongdoing, so if people are going to judge us unfairly, I guess there's not much we can do to stop 'em."

"So then…" Rachel dipped her head shyly. Arden had the urge to tuck her hair behind her ear so he could look into her eyes. "Does that mean you still want to take me to the pharmacy?"

"*Jah*, of course! And anywhere else you want to go."

As the horse clip-clopped along the country roads toward the *Englisch* superstore, Rachel chatted away about how she couldn't believe it had been ten years since she'd been in a buggy. She said she'd missed the rhythm, the pace, the sounds and even the smells of traveling that way. Arden sneaked a glance at her animated silhouette and grinned; her exuberance was charming.

Catching him looking at her, she said, "I'm babbling, aren't I? I assure you, it's not a post-concussion syndrome symptom."

"A what?"

"Oh, sorry. I was referring to symptoms that can be red flags after someone suffers a blow to the head. Like confusion or sensitivity to sound. Or like feeling a pressure to talk too much, the way I was just doing."

Arden's mouth went dry. "You think you have a c-con-concussion? It d-didn't seem like you h-hit your h-head when you fell, and th-the ground is so soft."

Rachel must have known she'd alarmed him, because she touched his shoulder. "*Neh!* I didn't hit my head, and I definitely don't have a concussion. It was intended as a joke because I'm jabbering so much. Nurse humor, that's all." She rested her hand on her lap again.

"Then what *do* you have that's making you gab so much?" Arden cracked.

"Well, it could be one of two things. It's possible I've *kumme* down with a bad case of homesickness— or I'm recovering from one. A person doesn't really know how much she's missed something until she has it again. Then she can't seem to get enough of it," she said, her voice quavering. Was that from the vibration of the carriage or something deeper?

"What's the other diagnosis?" he asked to lighten her mood.

"Too-much-sugar-itis." She grinned at him and confessed, "We had whoopie pies again for dessert."

He smacked his lips. "Now that's one illness I wouldn't mind catching."

Rachel lay in bed with her eyes closed, imagining herself in Arden's arms as he carried her from the backyard into the house. As terrified as she'd been by the moose attack—or pseudo-attack—she was equally enraptured by Arden's protective embrace. And his watchfulness hadn't stopped there; he'd persuaded her to give him the business phone that night because he wanted her to get a good night of rest and to sleep in as late as she needed the next morning. Even Arden's willingness to distance himself from her had been a demonstration of caring for Rachel, a way of looking out for her best interests, as well as those of her family. It was no wonder she was falling for him.

Rachel, you only think *you're falling for him*, she could hear Meg warning. *That's natural after someone saves your life. You know full well it's just a rush of hormones—dopamine, oxytocin, serotonin and endorphins. It will pass.* But that was exactly the problem; Rachel didn't *want* the feelings to pass. She wanted them to linger. She wanted them to *grow*.

Sighing, she rolled to her side. She couldn't wait to see Arden the next day. They had agreed if Ivan was well enough, she'd change places with Arden at lunchtime so she could paint the doghouse. As the rain thrummed on the rooftop, Rachel realized she'd never finished taking in the laundry. Now what would she do? Both of her skirts were on the line. She hadn't noticed until she was getting ready for bed that the back of the dress she'd worn tonight was dirty from when she'd fallen. She didn't want to knowingly go to work looking unkempt—especially in front of Arden.

That's when she remembered the lavender dress she'd begun sewing. She got up and padded downstairs to the living room. After checking on Ivan, she brought her fabric and sewing supplies back to her room. Stitching the dress again reminded her of the grape-suturing competition Toby had held against his brother. Maybe it was because she really *had* eaten too much sugar that evening, but the idea of suturing a patient repulsed Rachel to the point of nausea. Certainly she'd experienced queasiness before in her role as a nurse, but tonight she felt overwhelmed by it. *It's only nerves—a post-traumatic reaction to the moose scaring me*, she told herself.

Nevertheless, she tied a knot in the thread and clipped

it from the spool. Holding up the garment by its shoulder seams, she realized how closely it resembled the dresses she'd made as a girl. She hadn't intended to replicate the pattern—she hadn't even *used* a pattern—but with its long skirt, boxy top and clean, simple lines, it looked more like an Amish dress than an *Englisch* one. Amish women didn't use buttons or zippers on their garments, relying instead on straight pins or hooks. Rachel hadn't meant to imitate this practice, either, but sheer exhaustion caused her to abandon the idea of sewing a zipper into the dress, and she'd forgotten to buy buttons anyway. *This will have to do until I can rewash and dry my other clothes.* It was past two when she finally turned in and after seven when she woke the next day.

It was no longer raining, but the air was heavy with humidity and Rachel was glad she'd stayed up making the lightweight cotton dress. Since she'd be painting that day, she pulled her hair into a soft bun and then made her bed and went downstairs. To her relief, Ivan was still asleep—he'd stayed up until Rachel and Arden returned home the previous evening, which was much later than usual for him. Although she sensed he relished visiting with Grace as much as Grace did with him, Rachel hoped he wasn't overdoing it. She didn't want him to suffer a setback.

I might as well bring the laundry in, she thought, but she made coffee and swept the kitchen floor first. Then she swept the living room floor. After wiping out the fridge and reorganizing the pantry shelves, she recognized she was deliberately procrastinating going into the backyard. *That's silly. I'd be far more likely to encounter the moose again at dusk or dawn than at this time of day...*

She gathered her courage and stepped outside, nearly upending the laundry basket that was sitting in front of the door. Who knew she'd ever be so delighted to find a load of dirty linens and clothes! Arden must have collected them this morning. She brought the basket into the basement, and as the washer tub was filling, she examined the clothes. They weren't dirty, just wet from the night's rain—there was no need to rewash them after all. However, the sheet she'd been taking off the line when the moose disrupted her task was grimy along its edges where it had hung to the ground. Rachel filled the basin, added soap, put the sheet in the tub and turned on the agitator, allowing the machine to churn while she swept the basement floor. Afterward, she fed the sheet through the wringer and then carried it and the other items upstairs to hang on the line a second time.

But first she ducked into the bathroom to wash her hands, since they'd gotten dirty handling the sheet. Glancing at the mirror, she caught sight of her reflection and didn't immediately recognize it as her own. Upon taking a longer look at her lavender dress and Amish hairstyle, she gasped and promptly burst into tears as the past came rushing back. She didn't just recall how she'd *looked* before she left Serenity Ridge, but how she'd *felt*, how consumed she was with her dream of becoming a nurse. But she *had* become a nurse, so why was she crying now?

"Why are you crying?" Ivan's question from the hallway echoed hers.

She moved toward him, tears streaming down her cheeks. "I d-don't know—don't know who I am anymore." She hiccuped, her shoulders heaving.

"I do. You're my lovely *schweschder*," Ivan replied, which made her sob harder. He took her by her hand and led her to the couch in the living room, where he waited for her to stop crying before he brought her a glass of water.

She pushed a tear from her cheek with her wrist. "I'm the one who's supposed to be helping *you* feel better. You need your rest."

"*You* need *your* rest. Why don't you go back to sleep for a couple more hours?"

"I can't. I have to hang the laundry."

"It will still be there when you get up, because even if I had the energy, you wouldn't want me hanging it. It would end up more wrinkled than it is now."

Suddenly it occurred to Rachel to ask, "Who was doing your laundry before I got here?"

"Hadassah," he admitted sheepishly.

"But it's been years since they moved into their own *haus*."

"*Jah*. I told her she didn't have to do it, but I guess she didn't like the way I looked when I washed and hung out my clothes myself. Like I said, they somehow end up looking worse."

Rachel chuckled; say what she would about her sister-in-law, Hadassah had been looking out for Ivan for years, and in some ways, Hadassah probably thought of him as *her* little brother, too. "I'll hang the clothes first and then I'll go back to bed for a while. Just don't let me sleep past noon. I have a doghouse to paint."

As he worked alone for the third day straight, Arden tried to convince himself it wasn't Rachel in particular he missed—it was the silence that was getting to him.

But he knew that wasn't true; he'd been working alone for weeks when Ivan first came down with bronchitis, and the hours had never dragged on like this before. How was it that two weeks ago he'd never even met Rachel Blank and now, after only two and a half days without her in the workshop, Arden was keenly aware of her absence?

He kept scanning the area by the desk to catch sight of her chewing the end of a pen the way she sometimes did when she was reconciling the invoices, but of course she wasn't there. *I'd better get used to it*, he reminded himself. *In another few weeks, she'll be back in Boston.* And if Ivan didn't start regaining his strength, Arden wouldn't see Rachel very often until she left, either, because she'd continue to do the paperwork up at the house.

Even though they'd agreed she would paint the doghouse that day, Arden wouldn't be there at the same time—he'd be at the house with Ivan, since Rachel was concerned about him being too weak or becoming lightheaded and falling. *It's too bad her phone is broken, otherwise Ivan could use it to call the business phone if he needed help. That way, Rachel would be free to work here with me.*

Just then the phone's ringer cut through Arden's thoughts. He jogged across the workshop to pick it up as an Amish woman he didn't recognize breezed through the door. He held up one finger to indicate he'd be right with her, but as he pressed the phone between his shoulder and ear, Arden's attention was focused on jotting down the details for a change in the customer's order. Capturing the information on paper was a challenge, and it didn't help his concentration to have the Amish stranger hovering nearby. Arden had to ask the man on the phone to repeat the spelling of his last name twice, but even then he transposed the letters when he read them back to the customer. When Arden finally had it right, he said goodbye and snapped the phone shut, scratching out his errors while simultaneously asking the woman, "How may I help you?"

"I'm here to inquire if you construct fences, or only sheds."

"Only sheds and small buildings," Arden said, frowning at the square of paper. It was a mess; he hoped Rachel could read it.

"Oh, that's too bad. I've had a problem with a thirteen-hundred-pound trespasser in my backyard, and I heard your sheds are so durable I hoped you could build me an equally strong fence."

"A thirteen-hundred-pound tres—Rachel!" Arden dropped his pen. Her appearance had completely thrown him off. "I didn't recognize you."

She smiled. "*Jah*, I didn't recognize myself in the mirror, either. As you know, all of my other clothes had to be rehung. *Denki* for bringing them to the doorstep for me, by the way."

Arden couldn't concentrate on what she was saying. Although he'd seen her with her hair in a bun before and the dress she was wearing now wasn't all that different from the long *Englisch* skirts or modest dresses she normally wore, there was something about the simplicity of the ensemble that emphasized the uniqueness of her eyes. Previously he might have described them as almond shaped, but now he saw they were actually upturned and fringed with lashes that were thicker and longer at the outer corners. Even the little nick above her right cheekbone stood out against the plain backdrop of her outfit, enhancing the originality of her countenance.

She smoothed her skirt. "I know lavender is your least favorite color, but I won't be around much today, so you won't have to look at me in it for very long."

Arden hadn't realized he'd been staring. "I don't mind looking at you in it. I mean, I m-mean, the color is becoming on you. Or you are b-becoming in it."

The skin around her eyes crinkled with her smile— something else he hadn't noticed when she'd worn her hair down. "I might be wearing a polka-dotted dress by the time I'm done painting the doghouse, especially since I'll to have to hurry. I hope I can finish it quicker than you and Ivan can eat your lunch."

Arden couldn't stop himself from asking, "I, uh, I wa-was wondering if your cell phone works yet?" He presented his idea of giving it to Ivan so he could call her on the business phone if he needed help, which would allow her to spend more time in the workshop.

"Oh, that's a *gut* idea, but my cell phone has officially expired." She momentarily looked almost as disappointed as he felt, but then she brightened. "Hey! Instead of painting during your lunch break, I could go buy a disposable phone. I've wanted to get one while I'm here anyway. It doesn't feel right to use the business phone for my personal calls."

"That's a *wunderbaar* idea—"

Just then Grace entered the shop. "Oh, Rachel, your dress is lovely! Didn't I tell you? Arden, don't her eyes look pretty in that color?"

"Her eyes look pretty in any color." The words rolled off his tongue, and Arden couldn't tell who was most stunned by them—him, Rachel or his sister. Of the three, Grace recovered the quickest. She asked if they'd celebrate Ivan's birthday with her on Friday evening.

Rachel clapped her hand to her cheek. "I forgot his birthday is on the thirteenth!"

"I don't think he remembers, either—he said he's lost all sense of time. Which will make it more festive, kind of like a surprise party." After Rachel and Arden agreed a quiet celebration was in order, Grace said, "Today I've brought Ivan *hinkel supp* from *Mamm*. This morning I told her about the moose incident, so she also sent me off with a jug of chamomile sun tea to calm your nerves, Rachel."

"*Denki.* Ivan would probably like to have *supp* for lunch instead of the sandwich I fixed for him. You came at the perfect time if you'd like to join him and Arden at the *haus*. I have an errand to run."

"Actually, I need to get a smaller level—my three-foot one is too big for the shelves I need to hang in our next shed," Arden said. "So, I, uh, I'd like to go with you, Rachel. If Grace doesn't mind staying with Ivan, that is."

"That's fine," Grace agreed.

Arden didn't know if his sister's smirk was because it was obvious he wanted to spend time with Rachel or because Grace was pleased to visit Ivan alone again. *Probably both*, he decided, feeling a bit smug himself.

Rachel was glad she was wearing a long dress, because her knees were wobblier today from Arden's compliment about her eyes than they had been last night when the moose was coming her way. Fortunately, she was able to steady her hands against the steering wheel, and as she drove, she questioned Arden about Oneita's health.

"Her skin is so much better she doesn't want to go to the rheumatologist next week for her regularly scheduled appointment. Which reminds me, I was supposed to cancel it for her."

"Oh?" Rachel was concerned. "I'm not sure that you should do that. Her situation with her skin discoloration wasn't urgent, but it is something the *dokder* should be aware of so he can track it. He might want to make adjustments to her treatment plan, too."

"That's what I tried to tell her, but she thinks you gave her all the help she needs. And my *mamm* is as stubborn as…as a moose!"

Rachel giggled. "My *mamm* was like that, too. No one knew better than she did, because she was the *mamm*."

"*Jah*, that's why I was so surprised when my *mamm* listened to you." Arden added, "You must be very *gut* at talking to your patients because you're so considerate and easygoing, but you're very knowledgeable, too."

Rachel felt her cheeks flush. Two compliments from Arden in one day. That was more than she'd sometimes received from Toby in a month. "How about if I go talk to her before you cancel the appointment?"

Arden groaned. "She's going to think I put you up to it."

"*Neh*, she won't. Tomorrow when Ivan's asleep, I'll drop in casually to return her pitcher."

"*Denki.* I'd appreciate that."

"It'll be my pleasure." Building relationships with patients was one of Rachel's favorite parts of nursing, and she hummed the rest of the way to the superstore.

As they pulled into the parking lot, Rachel scanned the opposite corner. Since the Amish community was still small, there wasn't a covered area for horses and buggies the way there sometimes was in larger Amish communities. But in Serenity Ridge, the *Englisch* residents respected that the horses needed a quiet place where they wouldn't be disturbed, and someone had built a simple hitching post on the southernmost edge of the lot. Even though Arden had insisted the night before that he didn't mind if anyone saw them together, Rachel was relieved to find the area devoid of other Amish people. But in case any showed up, she suggested she and Arden separate inside the store and meet again outside at her car.

He wrinkled his forehead, his blue eyes dimming. "Don't you want to be seen with me? Are you afraid the *Englischers* will see you in that dress and assume we're courting?"

Flustered by the mere suggestion of Arden as her suitor, she stammered, "*Neh*, I just, I—it—it might take me a while because I've never bought a disposable phone before, so I have a few questions. I don't want you to stand around being bored."

"You mean because you'll be discussing technology and I won't understand it?"

"*Neh!* It's not that. I—"

Arden gave a satisfied grin; she hadn't realized he'd been jesting. "I'll go get what I need to purchase and then I'll meet you by the phones," he said.

Rachel's first order of business was to buy Ivan a birthday present, and she knew exactly what to get him: waders so next spring when he went fishing in Serenity Lake he wouldn't get so cold—which she suspected had played a role in his pneumonia *this* spring. After selecting a pair, she made her way to the electronics and technology section but couldn't find a staff person to help her, so she perused the back of the boxes of several different phones, comparing them. She'd narrowed her selection down to four possibilities by the time Arden arrived.

"Oh, wait—that one might be better," she said, indicating a phone on the shelf level with her chin. "Could you read me what that says about talk time and apps?"

Instead, Arden offered to hold on to the other four boxes so she could examine the fifth option herself. She was reading its list of features aloud when someone in the aisle interrupted.

"Is that you, Arden?" It was an Amish woman and a man who appeared to be her husband—or somebody's husband, because he wore a beard, as was customary for married Amish men. He also wore a neatly trimmed mustache, which was another anomaly practiced by the Amish in this part of Maine, as well as in a few other communities in the country. Unlike beards, mustaches weren't required for married Amish men living in Serenity Ridge—Colin and Albert had never grown them—but they weren't forbidden, either.

"Are you buying a phone?" the man asked, and Arden scrambled to set the boxes back on the shelf so quickly he dropped one of them on his toe. When he bent to retrieve it, he dropped it a second time.

For someone who supposedly isn't concerned about being seen with me, Arden sure is nervous, Rachel thought.

Of all the Amish people we'd run in to, it had to be the Rennos. Arden almost would have preferred to cross paths with Hadassah and Colin, because they would have ignored him and Rachel; Eva was going to ask a hundred and one questions.

"*Neh*. I'm not buying a phone. Rachel is." Arden felt like a schoolchild tattling on his classmate. "It's for her *bruder*, Ivan."

"Why does Ivan need a cell phone? Is it for work?" Eva asked him, as if Rachel weren't standing right there.

"He's going to use it while he's in the *haus* to call me at the shop if he needs me," Rachel said. She was making things worse by explaining. Even though Ivan was sick, most Amish people considered it unthinkable to use a phone at home, much less to use one to call a family member on their own property. "I'm Rachel Blank, by the way."

Whoops. Arden had been so surprised to see the Rennos he'd forgotten to introduce her, and after a pause he realized Eva and Ike weren't going to introduce themselves. "This is Eva and Ike Renno."

"*You're* the *Englisch schweschder*?" Eva questioned.

"That's not my *title*, but my *name* is Rachel, *jah*." Arden didn't blame Rachel for being annoyed to be referred to as the English sister, but her uppity tone wasn't going to win anyone over.

"Hadassah told us you were visiting. I guess she must have spoken to you about dressing appropriately in her *dochdere*'s presence."

"What?" Rachel's cheeks were going red, so Arden tried to steer the conversation in another direction.

"Eva's husband works with Colin and Albert," he said. "How *is* work, Ike?"

Eva wasn't to be deterred from her line of questioning, and she spoke over her husband. "I didn't see your buggy when I came in, Arden. Where did you hitch your horse?"

"I—I—I—"

"He rode with me in my car. It doesn't need a hitching post," Rachel quipped. Arden's one consolation was that Eva wouldn't catch on to her sarcasm.

"You left your workshop in the middle of the day to buy a phone?"

"And t-t-to get this," Arden said, displaying the level. It didn't occur to him to ask why Renno wasn't at work. "We're on our lunch break."

Eva looked at Rachel. "I was considering calling on Ivan. Arden told us he's had a terrible cough. I can make a honey-and-cider cough remedy that will stop him from hacking, although I'll have to drop by the organic market for honey on the way home."

"Oh, don't trouble yourself to do that," Rachel said.

Eva narrowed her eyes. "*Neh?* You only allow him to take *Englisch* medicine, is that it?"

"Not at all. Your remedy probably works as well— maybe even better—than an *Englisch* cough suppressant, but Ivan can't use one of those, either. You see, after having pneumonia, it's important he gets the *rotz* out of his lungs. It's *gut* for him to cough it up."

She wrinkled her nose. "I wasn't aware of that."

"You're *wilkom* to visit him any time, provided you haven't been sick. He's very susceptible to infection right now."

Eva huffed. "I'm *never* sick."

"*Gut*, then I hope to see you soon. For now, I need to find a sales clerk. As you mentioned, it's the middle of the day, and we need to get back to work." Rachel exchanged the box in her hand for one on the shelf, and after they both bid the Rennos goodbye, Arden followed her toward the customer service center.

Rachel couldn't believe the interaction they'd just had with Ike and Eva. What did she mean about dressing appropriately of front of Hadassah's daughters? Rachel had only seen little Sarah very briefly. "Wow, they really gave us the third degree," she muttered.

"What does that mean?"

Realizing the idiom in *Englisch* was foreign to Arden since the Amish rarely interacted with the courts or the police, Rachel chuckled. But before she could explain what she meant, Arden snapped, "There's no need to laugh just because I don't know that term."

"*Neh*, of course you don't," she acknowledged, surprised by how defensive he sounded. "It means they gave us a hard time. Interrogated us. Asked a lot of questions."

Arden didn't say anything most of the way home. Although he'd told Rachel he didn't care who saw the two of them together or what they thought if they did, she wondered if he minded more than he first let on. Not that she could blame him; Eva apparently was friends with Hadassah, and Rachel had a feeling Eva would repeat their conversation verbatim to her sister-in-law as soon as she could.

"You seemed a little nervous in the store," she finally remarked.

"What makes you say that?"

"Well, for one thing, you were stuttering a lot."

"That doesn't mean I was nervous," he barked.

Rachel was puzzled by his increasingly sour mood. Was he angry she'd implied a gossipmonger like Eva could make him nervous? If he wasn't irked because of the Rennos, it had to be because of something Rachel had said or done, but she didn't know what that might have been. "Have I upset you somehow?"

"I'm not upset," he said, scowling as they waited for the light to change. "If you're taking North Main instead of returning the same way we came, you'll have to turn right here. One of the drivers told me there's a detour because Fourth Street is washed out."

When Rachel put on her blinker and eased into the intersection, he frantically tapped the dashboard, saying, "*Neh*—other way!"

Waiting until she could safely change course, Rachel laughed nervously. "Someone who isn't upset doesn't mix up a simple thing like left and right. Do you want to tell me what's going on? Are you afraid Ike will tell Colin you were away from the workshop again? Or that you were buying a disposable cell phone?"

"I'm not *afraid* of anything. This trip was a necessity, not a social outing, and I'm on my lunch break. As for the phone, even if I was buying one, Colin would assume it's for my business. He knows I'd never flirt with buying technology for my own use. It's not as if I'm in danger of going *Englisch*."

That's exactly *what Colin would think and you know it, so why are you defending him all of a sudden?* Rachel was crushed. She couldn't comprehend why Arden was shutting her out like this, but maybe his behavior was the reality check she needed so she wouldn't continue to entertain the kind of ludicrous romantic notions she'd been having about the two of them.

"*Jah*," she said, crossing her arms against her chest. "I can't picture you going *Englisch* any more than I can imagine myself staying among the Amish."

Chapter Nine

Never in his life had Arden felt so humiliated. He stared out the passenger side window, stupefied by how Rachel had pointed out his stuttering, mocked him for mixing up left and right, and ridiculed him because he wasn't familiar with an apparently common *Englisch* phrase. And then, after insulting him, she had the good nerve to ask if anything was wrong!

But mostly, Arden was disgusted with himself for ever giving her the benefit of the doubt, especially after he'd overheard her talking on the phone. *Whether or not she was referring to me, she was calling* someone *dumb, and that should have shown me enough about her character to recognize how truly arrogant she is, no matter how unpretentious she appears on the surface.*

Not only had Rachel made fun of Arden, but she'd indirectly scorned the Rennos by rejecting Eva's offer to bring Ivan a homemade cold remedy. Eva might have been a blabbermouth, but her intention toward Ivan was kind. It wasn't as if Rachel actually had to administer the remedy to her brother, but why couldn't she have accepted it graciously instead of acting like a big show-off and delivering a lecture on phlegm? *If anyone should feel embarrassed, it should be* her, *not me!*

"I'm going to go show Ivan how to use this cell phone before I begin painting," she announced when finally they pulled to a stop in the driveway. Arden was already halfway out of the car.

"That's fine. I've got an errand to run. I've set the paint by the doghouse. The customer wants black trim, the rest in blue. I'll be back by three thirty or so." Then, as more of a demand than a statement, he added, "You should be finished painting by then."

"An errand? Why didn't you tell me?" Rachel questioned, her voice tremulous. "I could have taken you when we were out."

"I wanted to go by myself." Arden slid the rest of the way out of the car and shoved the door shut without a backward glance.

After getting his lunch bag from the workshop, he hitched his buggy and guided his horse toward Serenity Lake. It didn't matter to him how long he was gone; if necessary, he'd work from the time he returned until midnight rather than be in the same room with Rachel. Cutting across town toward the valley, Arden journeyed down a dirt road only the Amish were allowed to use, per the private landowner, to gain access to the water. After stopping at the edge of the woods to secure his horse, he followed the foot path to where the trees opened to a small clearing. There, jutting into the lake water loomed a boulder the Amish called Relaxation Rock, because its flat top was an ideal location for reclining. But Arden was far too wound up to relax. Pacing the narrow stretch of sand along the water's edge, he picked up a few stray stones and hurled them as far as he could into the sparkling clear lake.

As he chucked them, he snickered bitterly, thinking, *Too bad Colin and Hadassah or Eva and Ike aren't around to catch me playing hooky now.* He knew he should feel guilty, but he only felt tired out and fed up. His energy waning, he gripped the lunch bag between his teeth and scrambled to the top of the boulder. He ate his lunch slowly, reveling in the view until his eyelids grew so heavy he set his hat beside him, leaned back, folded his arms behind his head and fell fast asleep.

The last thing Rachel wanted was to be in the workshop when Arden returned, so she completed painting the doghouse as quickly as she could and cleaned the brushes and tray and put away the rest of the supplies. Then she gathered the ledger, a folder of invoices, two supply catalogs and the scheduling calendar, along with the business phone. From now on, she was going to stay far away from Arden for as long as possible. If he wanted her help, he was going to have to ask for it, because she was sick of volunteering and even sicker of his moodiness. *He wants to be by himself? Fine, he can be by himself. I'd rather run into the moose again than to cross his path!*

Thinking of the moose reminded Rachel she still had to take in the laundry. No sooner did she bring it inside than she changed out of the lavender dress and into her navy blue *Englisch* skirt and white blouse. As she put the dress she'd made on a hanger, Arden's compliment—"Her eyes look pretty in any color"—flitted through her mind, quickly followed by what he'd said about her being effective with patients. How could he go from saying such lovely things to behaving like such an oaf? The more she brooded about it, the more addled she became until she finally gave up trying to figure it out. *Why am I wasting my time speculating about Arden? Whatever happened to me being an independent and career-focused woman?* she chastised herself.

If only she could go to the bookstore to purchase the medical book on assessments and management protocols she'd been wanting to read, perhaps she could get her mind back on her future. But going to the bookstore would have meant leaving Ivan alone, and even though they both had phones now, Rachel was reluctant to be away from the house for that long. She'd noticed her brother's coloring looked off and she was convinced he was overly tired, especially later, when he turned in for the night at seven thirty.

As helpful as Grace had been by bringing meals and staying with Ivan in Rachel's absence, Rachel worried Ivan was sacrificing his sleep in order to visit with her. But how could Rachel broach the subject? The young couple were clearly in love. Besides, Grace was the only person who had come to see Ivan since he'd been discharged. Although he never mentioned this conspicuous lack of visitors, Rachel was disappointed by it. "That goes to show how wrong Arden was when he said the community would be *hallich* to help during Ivan's recovery," she said aloud to herself as she turned off the lights and went to sleep early, too.

Both she and Ivan were up at the crack of dawn the next morning, and he looked even livelier than Rachel did.

"You really don't have to stay at the *haus* with me today. You can go down to the workshop," he said when

Rachel returned from collecting eggs and milking the cow. "I'll be fine on my own."

"Something tells me you won't be on your own for long," Rachel absently replied as she counted the eggs. She was craving angel food cake but was one egg short.

Ivan chuckled. "You're right. Grace is stopping by with more *supp*. You and Arden should join us for lunch. I don't know how I'll ever eat it by myself."

"*Denki*, but since you'll have company, I'd like to go to town." It would be the perfect opportunity for Rachel to get the book she wanted. Maybe she'd even treat herself to an iced espresso and a muffin at the popular coffeehouse in town. Or buy eggs from the grocery store. She might even wear lipstick—no more plain dresses fastened with straight pins for her; Ivan was getting better, and Rachel needed to start acting like an *Englischer* again.

But her afternoon plans were thwarted when Ivan was taking a shower and Grace arrived with a large pot of soup in hand but wouldn't enter the house. Teary-eyed, she explained her mother had a mild fever again. "I don't know if it's a recurrence of her lupus symptoms or if she's coming down with something, but if it is an illness, it's possible I'll get it, or that I'm already carrying it. Which means I might have exposed Ivan to it!" she wailed.

Rachel took the pot and set it aside before calmly leading Grace to the porch swing. After asking about her mother's symptoms, as well as about her own health and hand-washing practices, she ventured Ivan didn't have much to worry about; Rachel's bigger concern was Oneita's lupus. Remembering she'd promised Arden she'd speak to his mother about keeping her upcoming doctor's appointment, Rachel provided Grace a face mask and asked her to stay with Ivan until she returned from checking on Oneita. By the time Rachel retrieved her keys and purse, Ivan had joined Grace in the kitchen, where she was setting bowls on the table.

"I'll be back soon. Remember, no kissing, you two—it spreads germs!" Rachel cautioned on her way out the door to make Grace and Ivan blush. Teasing her brother was something she'd never outgrow. Besides, she wanted to take advantage of the opportunity to prompt Ivan to ask to be Grace's suitor, if he wasn't already courting her. *Grace's* bruder *may be a grouch, but Grace is a* wunderbaar *woman.*

As she was getting into her car, Rachel spotted Arden helping an elderly couple load the doghouse into the back of a pickup. His curls were springs of light in the noon sun, and a damp spot bloomed across his bright blue shirt between his shoulder blades. As she watched him dexterously hoist the structure, Rachel remembered how he'd swept her into his arms after she fainted. She pinched her eyes closed to block the memory and exhaled heavily. When she opened them again, Arden was gone.

Arden stood by the desk, chugging down a cup of water. It was seeing Rachel as much as it was the humidity that had made his temperature rise. As steamed as he still was at her, he needed her help. In the past day alone, he'd received a dozen phone calls about orders, delivery dates and supplies, as well as a voicemail message from the bank requesting a return call. Even if Rachel had left the relevant paperwork behind, Arden still would have been hard-pressed to field the inquiries and process the information he was receiving. He just couldn't read and write fast enough, and he was tripping over his tongue more often than usual today, on account of having had insomnia the night before.

But apparently Rachel had somewhere to go—probably to an *Englisch* store, guessing by her appearance. She was back to wearing her usual clothes, and instead of pulling her hair into a neat bun, she'd piled it in a sloppy knot atop of her head. *She looks like she's been in a windstorm.* Arden instantly regretted the thought; by criticizing something as superficial as Rachel's wardrobe or hair, he was behaving no differently than Hadassah, and he liked to think he had far better reasons for finding fault with Rachel than that.

Then it occurred to him since Rachel had left the house, it was the perfect time to say hello to Ivan and drop off the notepad containing what little bit of information he managed to capture from the phone calls. To his surprise—he hadn't noticed his sister's buggy by the stable—Grace greeted him at the door wearing a blue mask. His pulse drummed in his ears; was Ivan okay?

"The mask is only a precaution," Grace said. "*Mamm* had a fever this morning, and since I've been in close contact with her, I was concerned I might accidentally transfer an illness to Ivan. Rachel said she doubts it, but she went to check on *Mamm* anyway. I guess she's going to try to convince her to keep her rheumatologist appointment, although I can't imagine *Mamm* will agree."

"I wouldn't be too sure about that—Rachel has a *gut* rapport with *Mamm*," Arden replied, automatically giving credit where it was due. Despite being miffed at Rachel, he was grateful she was going to try to persuade their mother to follow up with her doctor.

Because Rachel hadn't left an extra mask for Arden, when he entered the kitchen, he stayed across the room from Ivan. They chatted briefly before Arden handed off the information he'd brought with him.

"I ought to have Rachel bring me up-to-date on the paperwork," Ivan said. "But I'm afraid I sleep so much sometimes I don't know what actually happens and what I dreamed happened. I'm eager for things to be back to normal at the workshop again, though."

Not half as eager as I am, Arden thought. "No hurry. It's better not to push yourself. I wouldn't want you to relapse." *Especially if it means your* schweschder *would have to stay longer.*

Although Grace invited him to join them for lunch, Arden was too hot to eat soup and he didn't want to be there when Rachel returned, so he plodded back to the workshop. He had just crossed the threshold when the phone rang. *Not again*, he thought. This time the caller asked to speak with Rachel.

"She's not here at the moment, but how can I help you?"

The man chuckled. "You can't, except to give Rachel a message. Let her know Toby phoned and I'd like her to return my call as soon as possible. She's got my number. Thanks, guy," Toby said and disconnected before Arden could reply.

Thanks, guy? No wonder Rachel had dated Toby; he was just as condescending as she was.

"Hello, Rachel." Oneita patted the empty spot beside her on the double glider on the porch. "*Kumme*, sit. You look a little wan, dear."

Rachel tucked a strand of hair behind her ear. The

humidity was wilting her updo. "I may look as if I'm drooping, but I feel fine. How are *you* feeling?"

Oneita harrumphed. "Better than my *dochder* would have you believe. I assume she sent you here?"

Rachel laughed. "I was going to use the pretext of returning your pitcher, but I forgot to bring it. I would genuinely like to borrow an *oier*, though. But you're right, I came because Grace is worried about your fever."

"I honestly don't feel like I have one. I keep telling Grace she worries too much."

"I must say, you don't *look* sick. May I take your temperature?" Oneita agreed, so Rachel took a thermometer from her first aid kit and slid it beneath Oneita's tongue. When it beeped, she removed it and read aloud, "Ninety-eight point one. Nope, no fever."

"I knew that thermometer Grace was using was a piece of junk! I misplaced ours, so she picked up one on sale at the supermarket. I told her she was sacrificing quality for price, and this proves me right."

"I'm inclined to agree with you, but I can understand why Grace was worried," Rachel said diplomatically.

Even though no one else was anywhere around, Oneita lowered her voice. "I suspect she was even more worried about your *bruder* than about me. She's quite fond of him."

"I think Ivan's fond of Grace, too," Rachel confided.

"I reckon it's too early to plant celery for their *hochzich*, but I'd love to have Ivan as a son-in-law. He's been a blessing to our *familye*. Especially to my *suh*."

At the mention of Arden, Rachel shifted uncomfortably in her seat, but she acknowledged, "Ivan's very grateful to have Arden as his partner, too. I remember him writing to me that he was about to give up the idea of owning a business when Arden answered his ad. He was amazed a craftsman like Arden would relocate halfway across the country for an uncertain business endeavor."

"It must have been part of *Gott*'s divine plan for both of them, because your *bruder* gave Arden an opportunity he never would have had back home."

Despite being upset with him, Rachel's curiosity was piqued. "Really? Arden's so skilled—why wouldn't he start his own business in Indiana?"

"There are a lot of carpenters in that part of the country. They far exceed the demand. And of course, working in an *Englisch* job simply wasn't an option for Arden."

"*Neh*, of course not," Rachel murmured. Although she could understand why an Amish person might not want to work for an *Englisch* employer, hearing it still felt like an affront, especially since it was clear Arden would have preferred an Amish person to work with him during Ivan's illness, too.

Oneita continued, "He was crushed he couldn't work in the factory with his *daed*. But with Arden's reading and writing difficulties, well, he struggled through the application process, which included timed tests. And because his speaking problem is worse when he's tired or nervous, he didn't do well during the interviews, either."

His reading and writing difficulties? His speaking problem? It took a moment for it to dawn on Rachel. "Oh, you mean because he stutters sometimes? That doesn't seem fair for an employer to eliminate him for a job on that basis."

"His stuttering, *jah*, but it's more that he sometimes

has trouble getting his thoughts out. You've probably noticed it takes him twice as long to read and write as anyone else, too. That's why working with Ivan is such a *gut* fit for him. Your *bruder* handles all the calls and paperwork—and now you do, too. Although Arden is too self-conscious to talk about it, I know it was a huge relief when you arrived."

Rachel's stomach dropped, and if her skin hadn't already been clammy from the heat, she would have broken into a sweat upon remembering she'd asked Arden to read aloud from the phone packaging yesterday. She'd also pointed out he'd been stuttering. And laughed when he mixed up right and left. *No wonder he was so terse with me! He must think I'm a total jerk!* Her eyes stung, and she scrambled to her feet, causing Oneita to ask whether she was okay.

"*Jah*, but it occurred to me there's something I need take care of at the workshop." Rachel zipped to the car without another thought about borrowing an egg or even encouraging Oneita to keep her medical appointment—all that mattered to her now was making things right with Arden.

When Rachel barreled through the door, Arden was sitting at the desk finishing the last of his lunch while he puzzled over an order that had arrived in the mail. Ordinarily, he wouldn't have opened the envelope, but the customer had just called asking to change the specifications from those he'd written on his original request, which, unfortunately, included a variety of acronyms. Because Arden was too confused to make heads or tails of the order, he was forced to tell the customer he'd call him back later.

"I assume you've *kumme* for this." Arden pushed the rest of the mail across the desk toward Rachel. He stood and put his utensils into his lunch bag, which he dropped into the bottom desk drawer, and then he strode across the work area toward the sawhorses.

Rachel scampered in front of him. Peering up into his eyes, she clasped her hands beneath her chin and said, "*Neh*, I'm here to apologize, Arden. I'm so sorry for saying you seemed nervous the other day. And for calling attention to your stutter and the fact you mixed up the directions. I promise I wasn't making fun of you. I had no idea you have dyslexia."

Arden couldn't believe his ears. "Dyslexia? Who told you I have dyslexia?"

"Your *mamm*. She didn't use that word, but she told me about your challenges reading and writing. And about how you mix up letters—"

Arden didn't think it was possible to feel more embarrassed than he'd felt yesterday. But to discover his mother had discussed his...his so-called *challenges* with Rachel was too degrading for him to bear graciously. "So you diagnosed me with dyslexia? I thought a specialist had to do that. I thought there were tests involved. Or are you so uniquely qualified you can diagnose a person at a glance?"

Rachel's nostrils were turning pink, and her chin quivered. "*Neh*, you're right. I don't know for certain you have dyslexia. I just, I—I—I—"

"You're stuttering now. Is that because *you* have dyslexia?"

"Arden, I don't blame you for being angry at me, but I'm trying to make amends. I'm very sorry." Tears spilled from her eyes, but Arden was relentless. It was as if he was taking out all of the frustration and humiliation and fear of failure from the past nearly thirty years of his life on Rachel.

"What are *you* crying about? Does it t-take you t-ten minutes to read a simple passage from the Bible? How many t-times do you have to check your s-spelling for errors? Do you constantly w-worry you wr-wrote down a product code wr-wrong? Has anyone ever refused you a job or called y-you lazy when y-you were trying your hardest?" Arden was utterly exasperated that he couldn't even tell Rachel off without stammering. He ended by leaning forward and glaring at her as he asked, "Do *your* peers think *you're* stupid?"

She passed her arm across her face to wipe her tears away. "Sometimes, *jah*."

"Ha!" Arden scoffed, picking up a saw. "You? I doubt it."

"*Jah*, me," Rachel said, tapping her chest. "Not to the degree you've experienced, not even close, but I do know what it's like to try to prove myself to my peers. To know they think I'm not quite bright enough for them. To feel as if I don't measure up."

"That's a self-confidence issue. I have an *actual* problem with my abilities." He balanced a board across the two sawhorses.

"That might be true to a degree, Arden, but despite your struggles, you're one of the smartest, most creative people I've ever met. You'd have to be, to design such beautiful, unique sheds." Rachel gestured toward the side wall of the workshop. "You memorized where everything on every one of those shelves is. You retain more information in your head than I can capture in a logbook. And you knew exactly what questions to ask your *mamm* when I was trying to get to the bottom of what was triggering her skin discoloration. I didn't—and I'm trained in that kind of thing. It put me to shame."

As much as he wanted to believe Rachel meant what she said, Arden wasn't going to be fooled twice. "*Jah?* If that's what you really think, why did you tell someone on the phone how *dumm* I am, especially compared to Toby?"

"I never said such a thing! You must have misheard—oh." Rachel suddenly interrupted herself. She looked away, chewing her lip; Arden knew it. Despite what she'd just professed, she couldn't deny she'd called him stupid. "I didn't say you were *dumm*. I said you weren't *that* dull and—"

"So I should feel c-complimented because you said I'm not quite as stupid as you first thought?" Arden picked up the saw and began vigorously cutting into the board, his back to her.

"*Listen* to me, would you?" she shouted over the noise. "My roommate asked if you were acting morose because that was my original impression of you. But later, on the phone, I told her you weren't as dull as all that—*dull*, not *dumb*—meaning, you weren't so dreary. So morose."

Arden stopped sawing. He wanted to trust Rachel was telling the truth so badly his chest ached. He turned to face her. "You did?"

"*Jah*, I did." She added ruefully, "Although you're being so nasty right now I might change my mind again."

"Don't," he said, setting down the saw. He took both of her hands in his. "Please don't change your mind. I'm sorry. I—I—I've been trying to keep m-my difficulty a secret for so long. When y-you n-noticed it, I felt so… I thought you were being condescending. That you were looking down your n-nose at me."

"I could never look down my nose at you, Arden! I have nothing but deep respect and admiration for you."

He gently tugged her fingers, pulling her closer until they were only inches apart. "That makes two of us. I mean, I think that highly of you, too." His mouth went dry, and he licked his lips as she tilted her chin upward.

Rachel's legs turned to butter, and she felt her face flush beneath Arden's unflinching gaze. His eyes were bluer than blue, like the first patch of clear sky after a storm. As much as she wanted him to kiss her, Rachel couldn't let that happen—for his sake, more than hers. She forced herself to take a step backward and then she slid her hands from his grasp. He nodded in silent agreement and rubbed the perspiration from his forehead with the back of his hand.

Not two seconds later, the door creaked open. Arden jerked his head to the side, and Rachel spun around to see Jaala Flaud, the deacon's wife. *Wow, that was close!* Rachel thought, but her relief was short lived. *Uh-oh. She must be here to inform Arden the deacon and bishop want to speak to him about associating with me. Or worse, to suggest I leave Serenity Ridge.*

"So this is where you've been hiding!" Jaala exclaimed. "Rachel Blank, *kumme* give me a hug."

For an instant Rachel was too stunned to move, but then she nearly flew across the room into Jaala's open arms. As the deacon's wife enveloped her, Rachel inhaled the trace scent of nutmeg and cloves on her clothing. *The fragrance of my girlhood*, she thought, knowing Jaala must have made her renowned spice cake with cream cheese frosting that morning. Rachel whisked a tear from her cheek before letting her go.

Sizing Rachel up, Jaala remarked, "You look more like your *mamm* than ever. It is so *gut* to see you, but why did I have to hear about your arrival from Eva Renno? Nobody told me Ivan was out of the hospital, either."

"I'm sorry," Rachel replied. *And I'm sorry for assuming you wouldn't* wilkom *me back or visit my* bruder *while I was here, too.* "I assumed Colin or Hadassah would have told you."

"Ah, well, that doesn't matter now. We've got a lot of catching up to do. Will you join Abram and me for supper tonight? A few other young people will be there, too. There's plenty of cake for everyone. Arden, you're *wilkom* to *kumme*, too."

Rachel hesitated. "I'd love to, but I'm concerned about leaving Ivan—"

"I'll stay with him," Arden interjected.

"It's settled, then. We'll eat at six." Jaala linked arms with Rachel and started for the door. "*Kumme* with me while I visit Ivan. I figured since I'm one of the first to learn he's home, I'd better bring him a big vat of *supp*, and I need help carrying it in from the buggy."

Grateful but amused because Grace had already brought them so much soup they'd be eating it into next week, Rachel flashed a smile over her shoulder at Arden. When he winked and placed a finger to his lips, she wistfully thought, *That's not the only secret we'll have to keep to ourselves.*

Chapter Ten

"How is Ivan?" Rachel asked Arden when she returned from the gathering at Jaala's house. "Did he do his deep breathing exercises?"

"*Jah*. But he's tuckered out. He went to bed an hour ago."

"He needs as much rest as he can get. I meant to tell you I have to take him to a follow-up appointment tomorrow, so I'll only be in the workshop in the morning."

"That's fine. So, did you enjoy your visit?"

"It was *wunderbaar*. I met two couples—Maria and Otto Mast, and Sadie and Levi Swarey."

"Did you meet the Swareys' *kinner*, David and Elizabeth, too?"

"*Jah.*" Rachel giggled. "I had to remove a tick from David's scalp. Sadie was concerned he'll get Lyme disease, but I could tell by the tick's color and size it was a male and males don't transmit—Oh, I'm doing it again. I keep forgetting other people aren't as fascinated by these things as I am."

It occurred to Arden that Rachel hadn't meant to lecture Eva or to show off the other day—she was in the habit of sharing knowledge that was interesting to her and potentially helpful to others. "You're a natural teacher."

"*Denki.* Patient education is one of my favorite parts of nursing. They educate me by sharing what they've experienced, too." Rachel's voice lost its sparkle when she added, "Unfortunately, there's not much time to build relationships with patients in the clinic. We move 'em in and out. I spend more time entering data into their electronic health records than talking with the patients."

"Will that change when you become a nurse practitioner?"

"Ha! I'll probably have even *less* time."

"Yet becoming a nurse practitioner is what you want to do?"

"*Jah*, I suppose."

"Hmm."

"Hmm what?"

Somehow, now that Rachel knew about his trouble finding the right words, it was actually *easier* for Arden to express himself in front of her. "When you told me about becoming a nurse, you described it as a dream, almost an irrepressible one. You pursued that dream at great cost to yourself. That's a far cry from *supposing* you want to become a nurse practitioner."

Rachel chewed on the corner of her lip. There was a faraway look in her eyes but she simply shrugged and said, "*Jah*, well, maybe I won't get into the MSN program anyway."

"If you don't, you could always *kumme* back to Serenity Ridge for *gut*." Like most of his deepest-felt sentiments, this one sprang from Arden's lips, taking him by surprise.

Rachel seemed to think he was jesting. "*Jah*, I could ask Ivan to give me a job as painter in residence."

Arden attempted to cover the fact he'd been serious by kidding, "Or you could become Serenity Ridge's nurse in residence. We Amish need someone to lecture us about *rotz* and ticks and the dangers of cough suppressants."

"Lecture?" she asked. "You mean the other day? Was I really that bad? The only reason I told Eva not to bring the cough remedy was because she was going to buy honey from the expensive organic market just for that purpose, and I didn't want it going to waste."

I've really misjudged her, Arden realized again. "*Neh*, you're not *that* bad," he said, blithely imitating her tone when she said he wasn't *that* dull.

"Gee, thanks." She gently pushed on his bicep, frowning in mock consternation. How he wished he could kiss that fake pout from her lips... Her cell phone rang, and Arden wrenched backward. She pulled it from her purse and glanced at the display screen. "I'd better answer this. *Denki* for staying with Ivan. I'll see you in the morning?"

"See you in the morning," Arden echoed as she lifted the phone to her ear. Rachel had already shut the door behind him when he remembered he'd never told her that Toby had called that afternoon. *Maybe that's him on the phone with her now. Maybe he's wondering when she's coming home*, Arden conjectured. *What if he's calling because he wants to date her again?* He didn't know what had inspired that idea, but once he got it into his head, it was all he could think about.

* * *

"Guess who's going to be a nurse practitioner?" Meg taunted in a singsong voice.

"Who?" Rachel's mind was still on her conversation with Arden. *Was he serious about wanting me to stay in Serenity Ridge?*

"Do you really have to ask? *You* are, that's who. You got into the MSN program!"

"I did?" Rachel had been anticipating the university's decision for so long she thought she'd be exuberant when she finally heard, but instead she felt hollow.

"Yes, you did!"

"Oh." Her eyes filled with tears—and they weren't the happy kind, either.

"Oh? That's all you have to say? What's wrong? Aren't you glad you got in?"

"Yeah, I am," Rachel said, but Meg could tell she wasn't being completely honest.

"That answer lacks conviction, Rach. What's going on? Has Ivan had a relapse?"

"*Neh*, Ivan's definitely improving. It's just that, it's just…it's *everything*," Rachel cried, releasing a torrent of pent-up emotion. Meg listened to her recount a hodgepodge of anecdotes, from nearly being trampled by the moose to her argument and subsequent reconciliation with Arden to the lovely evening she'd just enjoyed at the deacon's house. She also lamented Colin and Hadassah's behavior, the fact her nieces and nephews hadn't known she existed, and the realization she'd wrongly made assumptions about the Amish community in Serenity Ridge. She ended by saying how conflicted she'd felt lately about becoming a nurse practitioner. "To be honest, I don't think I want to *be* a nurse practitioner as much as I wanted to prove I *could* be one. And I especially wanted to prove it to Toby. It was a matter of pride—what the Amish call *hochmut*."

"I'm not entirely surprised—you love nursing so much, I never really could imagine you changing roles. As grueling as the application process was, at least you figured out you don't want to go through with becoming an NP before you enrolled in the program or quit your job," Meg consoled her. "For a minute there, I was afraid you were going to tell me you weren't coming back to Boston…"

Rachel hesitated a spell before assuring her, "No, I'm coming back."

"Good, because I miss you. The only bad thing about returning is that you'll still have to work with—oh no!" Meg abruptly exclaimed. "I forgot to tell you. Toby called the other day. Please don't be mad, but I gave him your number. The one at the workshop, I mean."

"Meg!" Rachel groaned.

"I'm sorry, Rach, but he left me, like, five messages. When I finally picked up, he told me he and Brianna broke up and he seemed desperate to talk to you. I figured he was going to call and beg you to take him back and I, well, I kind of wanted you to have the satisfaction of telling him no way… And, hey, now that you've found out you got into the MSN program, you can rub his nose in that, too, even if you aren't going to enroll."

Rachel sighed. Two weeks ago she would have derived a certain satisfaction in spurning Toby or telling him she'd been accepted into a top-notch MSN program, but now she had no desire to do something so vengeful and vain. "I'll talk to him if he calls, but I'm not going to tell him about getting into the program."

"I know, I know," Meg muttered. "The Amish would consider that to be *hallich maage*."

"Hallich maage?" Rachel repeated.

"Yeah. Pride."

"You mean *hochmut*."

"What did I say?"

"It sounded like *hallich maage*, which loosely translated means *happy stomach*." Rachel giggled.

"Don't poke fun at me or I'll remind you of the time you called a phlebotomist a *lobotomist*."

The two roommates cracked up as they reminisced about other humorous things Rachel had said or done while she was acclimating to the *Englisch* lifestyle. Before they bade each other goodbye, Rachel told Meg to give Toby her temporary cell phone number if he called again—she didn't want him using the business phone.

She got ready for bed, but long after midnight, Rachel lay awake, mulling over Arden's suggestion that she might return to Serenity Ridge for good. It wasn't as if the idea hadn't occurred to her already, but as Meg had accurately pointed out, Rachel loved being a nurse. And as Arden had reminded her, she'd sacrificed so much to become one. *But if I love nursing so much, why do I feel so discontent when I imagine returning to my job in Boston?*

On Friday morning, Arden kept watching the door. Rachel hadn't been coming in as early as she did before Ivan was discharged, and he was eager to tell her about the phone call from Toby, which had been weighing heavily on his mind. Besides, he liked being in Rachel's company as often as he could.

She eventually ambled in at nine thirty, whistling.

When Arden relayed the message, she didn't seem surprised. "Sorry about that. Meg gave him the business phone number," she said, which made Arden even surer Toby had been in touch with Rachel already. Was he also right in guessing what they'd spoken about?

It's none of my business, he reminded himself. "I've got two customers arriving shortly to discuss modifications to this shed," he informed Rachel, pointing at the structure. "If you'd listen to the rest of the voice-mail messages, I'd appreciate it. We had several I didn't attend to yesterday."

"Of course," she agreed and lifted the business phone from the desk. Her smile was especially winsome this morning, and Arden could no longer keep himself from fishing to find out why.

"Your eyes are gleaming. Have you got a secret?" he hinted.

She stopped tapping on the cell phone to squint at him, her head cocked. "As a matter of fact, I do."

"Do you want to share what it is?"

"Jah..." she stalled, looking at the phone again. "But not now. You'll find out at Ivan's birthday party."

Clearly she was being coy, and while Arden might ordinarily have enjoyed this kind of badinage, today it felt like torment. He shamelessly pleaded with her. "I'm really *gut* at keeping secrets if you want to tell me now."

"Well, I could but then—"

The couple Arden was expecting entered the workshop, enthusiastically greeting Arden before Rachel could complete her sentence. She gave him a one-shouldered shrug and a puckish smile, as if to say, *Oh, well.* Resigned to bearing the suspense until the couple left, Arden led them to the shed, where he listened to their proposed design modifications.

As they spoke, Arden glanced over at Rachel, who was frantically flipping through the ledger with one hand and holding the phone to her ear with the other. She must have slipped out the door a few minutes later, because the next time he looked up, she was gone. After the couple departed, he found a note on the desk reading, *Arden, I had to run an errand. I won't be back this afternoon since Ivan has his MD appointment. I took the phone in case a customer calls. I'll see you tonight at six.* She'd signed her name, and next to it she'd sketched a moose's head. The moose was winking, and beneath him she'd scrawled, *You* moose *not try to guess my secret—it will spoil the surprise!* And despite his impatience to find out her news, Arden had to laugh.

I've gone over the ledger so many times I was sure it was correct, Rachel thought as she drove to the bank. But obviously it wasn't, otherwise the bank manager wouldn't have left so many voice-mail messages the past couple days. The first were simply requests to return his calls, but in this morning's message he informed her there were insufficient funds in the business account to cover the check Ivan had written to the hospital. Because Blank's Sheds was a longtime customer in good standing, the manager was contacting Ivan as a courtesy, allowing him until noon today to reconcile the deficit in order to avoid bouncing the check and incurring a fee. Even more worrisome was the possibility the hospital might rescind the discount on Ivan's bill if it wasn't paid in full immediately, as agreed.

As she stopped at a traffic light, Rachel remembered

Arden mixing up right and left, and it occurred to her *he* might have been the one who made an error in their records. *Everything was balanced perfectly when my brother relinquished the accounting responsibilities to Arden, so it couldn't have been Ivan's doing.* Aware that sometimes people with dyslexia also had dyscalculia, Rachel wondered if that was the case with Arden. She dreaded telling him about the error, anticipating how self-conscious he might feel.

And the timing was terrible—tonight she'd planned to confide in him, Ivan and Grace that she'd been accepted into the MSN program but wouldn't be enrolling. She had stayed up praying about it throughout the night, and she knew it was the right decision, but she was less certain about her other unshakable idea: *Maybe I should stay in Serenity Ridge permanently.* Tonight she wanted to test the waters, to hear if her brother and her new friends thought that was a plausible option.

For now, her sole objective was to prevent Ivan's check from bouncing. By speaking to the manager in person, she hoped to buy more time. Although he'd said the account was several thousand dollars short, Rachel prayed there might be a check from a customer in today's mail that would cover the deficit. Then, right before turning into the bank parking lot, she was struck by another solution: she could transfer the funds from her own account. Now that she wouldn't have to pay tuition fees, she couldn't think of a better use for her savings. She was thrilled when the manager accepted her proposal, not merely because it resolved Ivan's business problem, but also because it seemed like further affirmation that she'd made the right decision about the MSN program.

After contacting her bank and arranging for the transaction, she barely had enough time to get home and take Ivan to his appointment. The doctor said he'd made remarkable progress; his oxygen saturation level had come up, and his lung X-rays looked better, too. "You must be very committed to practicing your breathing exercises, aren't you?" the doctor asked.

"Not half as committed as my *schweschder* is to *making* me practice them." Ivan's comment made the doctor chuckle.

"I wish all my patients had someone like your sister to take care of them. You're very fortunate."

"That's true. I don't know what I would have done without Rachel," Ivan said, beaming at her.

It was such a relief to hear about Ivan's improved health and she was so eager to share her decision not to become a nurse practitioner that Rachel decided she'd wait until the following day to discuss the insufficient funds issue with Arden.

As it turned out, that evening Rachel discovered she'd have to wait to tell everyone about her career decision, too, because every time she tried to bring up the subject, she was delayed. First, Grace was upset because she overcooked the roast. It was so tough they ended up having soup—again. Rachel chose not to tell everyone immediately after supper because she wanted the focus on her brother as he opened his gifts. Then, as they were eating cake, Ivan suffered a coughing fit that was so extreme Rachel suggested he'd benefit from a steaming bath. Ivan reluctantly agreed, and Grace began stacking the dessert dishes, but it was Arden who dragged his feet about leaving. He had seemed so agitated all evening—squirming in his seat and picking at his food—Rachel was surprised he wanted to linger.

"I, uh, know Ivan needs his rest, but first don't you have news to share, Rachel?" he asked.

She smiled. "*Jah*, I'm glad you asked about that. I—" As she was speaking, the business cell phone vibrated on the coffee table where Rachel had left it so Arden would remember to take it home since he was expecting an early-morning call the next day. Rachel leaned forward to check the number. "I don't need to get that. What I was going to say is that I've decided to—"

Immediately after the business phone stopped vibrating, Rachel's phone began ringing from atop of the desk in the corner. Rachel crossed the room and picked it up. "It's Toby. He's going to keep calling until I answer, so give me one sec," she said before ducking into the kitchen.

"Ivan, you look miserable," Grace cooed. "I wanted our gathering to be special, but I'm afraid this party might have set your recovery back three weeks!"

"Don't be *lappich*. I'm sorry my coughing cut our celebration short. The party was so thoughtful—and I was genuinely surprised."

Arden shifted in the chair, feeling like a third wheel as Ivan and Grace unabashedly exchanged sentiments of affection. From where he sat he could hear bits of Rachel's phone conversation with Toby. He caught phrases like "I've already forgiven you," and "what I want more than anything." *I knew it*, he thought, his suspicions confirmed. Rachel had reconciled with Toby.

"Can't you, Arden?" Grace questioned, jolting him back to their conversation.

"Sorry, what did you say?"

"I said, can you take Ivan to *kurrich* and back home on Sunday? He shouldn't be on his own, and I'll be going with *Mamm* to visit Aquilla King." Aquilla was a childless widow who had recently had hip surgery, and as was customary, the female members of the Amish community were either taking turns staying with her or bringing meals to her home.

"*Jah*, of course," Arden agreed, adding that since Rachel might be a while, he and Grace should leave so Ivan could take his bath. Since they were traveling in separate buggies, Arden said goodbye before Grace did. He retrieved the business phone from the coffee table and tried to creep past Rachel in the kitchen, but she excused herself from Toby and covered the phone with her hand.

"I'm sorry about this," she said, indicating the phone. "I'll tell you my news tomorrow."

"No hurry." Arden wasn't in a rush to hear her announce she was getting back together with Toby. *It doesn't make a whit of difference to me either way*, he thought bitterly, even though he'd been consumed by the possibility all day long…and even though the reality kept him rolling from one side to the other throughout the night, too.

In the morning he was surprised when his mother told Grace that Tuesday was their turn to spend a day and night with Aquilla.

"Tuesday? That's when you have your appointment with the rheumatologist," Arden reminded her.

"You were supposed to cancel that for me."

"I didn't because… Didn't Rachel talk to you about it?"

"*Neh*. Why would she? If the *dokder* doesn't receive

forty-eight business hours' notice for cancellations, they charge a fee. Now I *have* to keep the appointment. I hope I can find someone to switch days with me at Aquilla's *haus*," his mother fretted. "I wish you would have kept your word, Arden."

"I'm sorry, *Mamm*," Arden apologized, begrudgingly wondering why Rachel hadn't kept *her* word to speak to his mother. Then he remembered: the two women had probably been too busy discussing his so-called dyslexia. *Oh well, that's water over the dam now,* he conceded. *At least* Mamm*'s still going to the doctor.*

When he got to the workshop, Arden received the call he'd been expecting. Before disconnecting, the customer informed him he'd tried to leave a message the evening before, but the voice-mail box was full. So Arden listened to the old messages to determine which ones he could safely delete. That's when he heard it: an urgent warning from the bank manager indicating they had until noon on Friday to avoid bouncing the check Ivan had written to the hospital. *How could we be short that much?* Arden was stumped, and his hairline and upper lip beaded with sweat. *Rachel assured me we were in the black.*

He opened the ledger and did his best to review the entries, but there were so many abbreviations and acronyms his vision blurred. Whatever had happened, it had to be his fault, since Rachel was fastidious about her calculations. But how could anything he'd done cause such a big discrepancy? Since Ivan had been sick, Arden had only written a handful of checks, and those were never for more than a couple hundred dollars—with the exception of the check he wrote to Knight's for the cedar two-by-sixes. But he'd told her about that and surely she'd recorded it, hadn't she?

His hands trembling, he thumbed through the ledger, scanning it first for the figure, which was easier for him to recognize than the product code. It wasn't there. He searched again and again one more time, unable to believe Rachel hadn't recorded it. *No wonder she thought we had more than enough funds to cover Ivan's bill.* At the time, Arden hadn't understood how that could possibly be the case, but since he was used to being the one to make errors and Rachel was so smart, he assumed she'd been right. Now he almost wished he *had* been the one who'd made the mistake. Rachel was so conscientious about protecting Ivan's health; she was going to be devastated to learn she'd caused harm to his business. Even worse than being charged an overdraft fee and blemishing their record at the bank was the possibility the hospital might not allow a discount now, since the check had bounced. Arden shut his eyes and prayed, *Please, Gott, if it's not too late, help me think of a solution to prevent that from happening.*

"Somebody must have stayed out too late last night," Rachel said, gently touching his shoulder. "Were you asleep or are you coming down with something?"

"Neh, I—I—I," he stuttered. "I'm afraid I have something upsetting to discuss with you." To Arden's surprise, after telling her about the bank, Rachel smiled.

"Phew. I thought you were going to tell me your *mamm* was sick. I've already covered the deficit. It's all set for now."

"Y-you covered it? C-covered it, how?"

Rachel picked at her thumbnail. "I transferred funds from my personal account. I, uh, I'd been saving up for tuition, but, well, my big news was that I decided I don't want to go back to school, so… I was in a position of being able to cover the deficit."

As relieved as he was the business wouldn't be fined and the hospital would be paid on time, Arden felt profoundly disappointed Rachel had tried to hide her mistake like that. Why hadn't she told him about it? Was she too proud to admit she made an error? "When were you going to *kumme* clean about this?"

"*Kumme* clean?" Rachel narrowed her eyes. "You make it sound as if I should be ashamed. I wasn't trying to deceive you, Arden. I was trying to *help* you. Sometimes when people struggle with language or reading and writing, they also have challenges with math and I didn't want you to feel bad. Especially because we were celebra—"

"Whoa!" Arden sputtered. "You are unbelievable! You assume because I have a problem with words, this accounting error has to be my fault, too?"

"*Neh*, I didn't assume this was your fault because of anything other than the fact I've scrutinized the figures in the ledger a dozen times and everything adds up, so this had to have been an error that occurred before I got here. It couldn't have been Ivan, since he was ill, so it had to be you."

"Of all the condescending, self-satisfied, disparaging things you've ever said, *that* takes the cake!" Arden jumped up and stomped halfway across the workshop before he stopped, swiveled around and shouted, "Let me tell you something, lady! Even if I had made an error, I don't need you to protect me from the truth. I've been making errors and living up to the consequences most of my life! Trying to protect me from my own mistakes is not how you treat a man—it's how you treat a *kind*. Or someone you pity."

"I wasn't going to keep it from you, and I wasn't being condescending," Rachel cut in. "I covered the deficit because I care about you and Ivan and your business."

She tried to say more, but Arden wouldn't let her. "You want to know the great irony here, Rachel? I actually did think I was the one who made the error. That was my first thought—and apparently, it was your first thought, too. But here's the kicker—*you* were the one who made the mistake. It was *your* fault, not mine, so don't you dare act as if you were doing *me* any favors!"

Rachel pulled her chin back, her eyes wide with bewilderment. "*My* fault?"

"*Jah*, as hard as that might be for you to accept. You never recorded the payment I made to Knight's for a surplus shipment of two-by-sixes after I expressly asked you to."

She shook her head and furrowed her eyebrows. "I don't remember you asking me to do that—"

"*Neh*, and you didn't remember to talk to my *mamm* about keeping her appointment, either. But one thing I *can* do better than you, Rachel Blank, is remember. You were sitting right there at that desk and I told you we had a delivery from Knight's and we got a 10 percent discount. I said I wrote out a check but I didn't record the amount in the ledger yet. Then I said Mrs. McGregor wanted the playhouse completed a week early and I asked you to call our delivery guy and arrange for that. *Now* do you remember?"

Parts of what Arden said were vaguely coming back to Rachel, but his tirade was so venomous she could hardly think straight. "I suppose some of that sounds familiar," she said meekly.

Arden pounced on that, his voice booming through the workshop, "*That's* all you have to say for yourself? Not *I'm sorry*, not *I was really wrong*?"

"You aren't giving me a chance! And even if I did apologize right now, you wouldn't accept it. There's nothing about your demeanor that suggests you want to work this out—your entire intention is to tell me off. To put me in my place," she yelled back. "Well, let me tell *you* something, mister—for someone who's supposedly so humble, you're being thoroughly contemptuous!"

"And for someone who's supposed to be so *schmaert*, you're as dense as a brick!" Arden hurled the insult at her. "How did you ever manage to get into an MSN program when you can't even remember something as simple as telling a patient to go to the *dokder*?"

Her voice dripping with sarcasm, Rachel sniped, "Gee, Arden, I don't know. Maybe the *Englisch* are just more forgiving of my mistakes than the Amish are."

Arden's face was so red it was tinged with blue. "Then maybe you should just go back to the *Englisch* already, because as we've all seen, you don't fit in here!"

"I'd rather fit in with *Englischers* who are forgiving than Amish hypocrites like you and my *bruder* and sister-in-law," Rachel retorted before she spun on her heel and tromped out, slamming the door behind her so hard the building shook.

Chapter Eleven

Too angry to drive and too upset to let Ivan see her in this state, Rachel couldn't go back into the house, so she marched across the lawn toward the edge of the property. She and her brothers had blazed a trail through the woods leading from their house up a rocky incline to the southern end of the ridge that inspired Serenity Ridge's name. The path wasn't as well-worn as when Rachel left, so she found a large stick and hacked away at the spring underbrush, her vision blurred with tears.

How could I have ever imagined I was falling for Arden—or wanted to kiss him! He's even more critical than Toby, Rachel thought as she progressed deeper into the forest. Even if she'd made a mistake with the bookkeeping, she'd covered the deficit with her own money, so she would have thought he'd be grateful for her help, not pious about her error. She yelped as a black fly bit her upper shoulder; she'd forgotten how much pain those little critters could inflict. *That's one more thing I won't miss when I go back to Boston.*

Recalling Arden saying she didn't fit in and suggesting she leave now, Rachel shoved a thick tree limb off the path with her heel. *Nothing is going to get in the way of where I want to go or what I want to do*, she thought. But where and what *was* that? Just last night she'd imagined not only staying in Serenity Ridge indefinitely but rejoining the Amish and being baptized into the church. She'd even hinted at her plans to Toby over the phone.

He'd begun their conversation apologizing for dating Brianna behind Rachel's back and then asked if she'd consider seeing him again. Rachel said she'd already forgiven him, but that she wasn't interested in a relationship; that's when she let it slip she was contemplating staying in Maine among the Amish permanently.

He'd argued, "You can't live up to your potential there, Rachel."

"*Neh*, I can't live up to *your* expectations of me here," she countered. "But I *can* try to follow *Gott*'s plan for my life. And that's what I want more than anything."

"But you love being a nurse. You've said it hundreds of times."

"I think… I think I love being Amish more. Besides, I can still take care of people in my family and community in an unofficial capacity."

"You mean without getting paid for it?"

"There are more important things in life than money and prestige, Toby," Rachel scolded, only half-seriously. She knew Toby had deep faith in God, even if his recent behavior had been less than honest.

"Like what, sticky buns and *yumsetta* casserole?" he grumbled.

"Exactly!" Rachel laughed, glad they were ending things on a better note the second time around, and saying her intention aloud made her gain confidence she was on the right track—returning to her Amish roots seemed to be what the Lord was leading her to do.

Her own words came back to her now: "I think I love being Amish more." The problem was, as Arden so cruelly pointed out, the Amish apparently didn't love her. Or at least, several of the Amish people she cared most about—which until today had included Arden—didn't want her around.

She slapped her neck, and a fly fell to the ground. A few feet ahead, a tree had fallen across her path, and she didn't know whether to climb over it or turn around and go back. *Where* am *I anyway?* She thought she knew, but now she wasn't so certain. Once, after she'd gotten lost in the woods as a girl, Colin had told her if it ever happened again, she should sit down and wait to be rescued. Too hot, itchy and tired to continue, Rachel leaned against the fallen tree. *Lord,* she prayed, *please guide my next steps*—all *of them.*

After a couple of hours, Arden's temper had cooled enough that he was able to devise a plan so he wouldn't have to work with Rachel any longer. First chance he got to speak to Ivan alone, he was going to tell him what Rachel had done. Her mistake could have cost their business and their reputation—with the hospital, as well as the bank—too much to allow her to continue managing the paperwork and bookkeeping. As an equal partner, Arden had decided it was time they either hired a temporary *Englisch* administrative assistant or recruited someone from the Amish community. *Who knows, Rachel's so arrogant this change might offend her so much she'll decide she's leaving Serenity*

*Ridge before Ivan recovers. If so, Grace will be able
to take care of him now that* Mamm *is well again...*

The more he thought about his plan, the more anxious he became to implement it. He would've gone to the house and told Ivan right then if it weren't that he couldn't stand the sight of Rachel. As it turned out, Ivan rambled into the workshop right before he left for the day at one o'clock. Arden figured Rachel had already given her brother her skewed version of what occurred.

"Feels *gut* to be in here again," Ivan said, inhaling. "Rachel's concerned about the sawdust irritating my lungs, but I've missed the smell. Where is she, anyway?"

Arden scrunched his forehead. "She left here a couple hours ago. I thought she went to the *haus*."

"*Neh*, and her car's still in the driveway."

"She must have gone for a walk. She, uh, was kind of upset. She made a pretty big error," Arden began. He delved into an account of what had transpired with the check for the hospital bill as impartially as he could, sticking to the details and refraining from suggesting they replace Rachel until Ivan had a chance to absorb the gravity of her mistake.

"You think my *schweschder* was upset she had to use her money to cover our deficit?"

Arden was surprised it didn't seem to be sinking in. "*Neh*, she said she had that money available because she decided not to enroll at the university. Besides, we'll pay her back. I think she was embarrassed she made such a potentially destructive mistake. And I have to confess, I expressed my displeasure she didn't tell me about it sooner."

"*Jah*, that was a big burden for her to bear on her

own. I wish she would have told *me*, too. I suppose since we put her in charge of bookkeeping, she must have felt responsible for straightening it out with the bank manager."

Arden was dumbfounded; couldn't Ivan understand how careless Rachel had been? "I think it might be time to find someone else to manage our accounting."

"I agree. Someone who doesn't care about me— about *us*—so much wouldn't have given up their savings like Rachel did. I'd rather we hire an *Englisch* stranger than put her in that position. The only thing that puzzles me is how we got so far behind in the first place. You've been filling orders day and night, according to Rachel. Have customers been remiss in paying us?"

Arden felt as if he'd been whacked upside his head with a two-by-four. No—a two-by-*six*. And well he should have, for tearing into Rachel when the very reason she'd had to cover the debt was because of the mistake *he'd* made first. "I, uh, I'm afraid I, uh, ordered too much cedar. It set us back and I—I—I—I didn't want to have to pay the return fee, so I accepted the delivery."

Ivan nodded slowly. "Ah, I see. Well, we all make mistakes, and I'm sure we'll use the wood and profit from it soon. We'll work with Rachel to figure out a suitable repayment plan meanwhile."

"Jah," Arden said, but in light of Ivan's grace, he felt so ashamed the word was barely audible.

"Anyway, I came to tell you your *schweschder* called Rachel's cell phone from the phone shanty. She tried to call here but kept getting voice mail."

"I didn't hear it ring. Is my *mamm* okay?"

"Jah, but the two of them are making *supp* to take to

Aquilla tomorrow, and they want you to pick up a set of freezable containers."

"Okay," Arden agreed. But his feet were leaden as he put away his tools and swept up the sawdust. His heart was heavy, too, with the awareness that every single insult he'd cast at Rachel—that she was condescending, self-satisfied and disparaging—was doubly true about *him*.

He dropped to his knees on the hard concrete floor. *Lord, I've been so proud and self-righteous. Please forgive me. Please help me to make amends with Rachel, and for her to forgive me, too. Wherever she is right now, please protect her heart from the rancor of my words.*

By the time Rachel returned home, she had a dozen fly bites on her neck and face, her dress was damp with sweat, and she was parched. She assumed Ivan would be taking his afternoon nap, but instead he threw open the screen door the moment her foot touched the first step.

"Rachel, I've been worried sick about you!" His sentiment caused her to break down in tears—at least *one* person in Serenity Ridge loved her. He insisted she sit on the porch swing while he brought her a glass of water and a cold compress. Sitting beside her, he wrapped his arm around her shoulders.

"I'm smelly," she apologized, but he drew her closer.

"Arden told me what you did for us. I'm grateful, Rachel—but also sorry you felt so responsible as to take on our debt. I promise we'll pay you back as quickly as we can."

While it didn't surprise her that Ivan had a different response to her actions than Arden did, she wondered what Arden had told him about their heated exchange. "I know you will, but as I said to Arden, I couldn't think of a better use of my savings than putting the money toward your hospital costs. I'd do it again in a heartbeat."

"But are you absolutely certain you don't want to become a nurse practitioner?"

"I've never been more certain about a decision in my life—except when Toby asked me to get back together last night and I said *neh*," she replied. *It's the decision about whether or not I should stay here I'm confused about.*

"He did?"

"*Jah*, but can we talk more about this later? I need to take a shower."

"You do that, and I'll warm some *supp*. We'll have an early supper."

Rachel groaned. "I don't know if I can swallow another spoonful of *supp*. Do you suppose you'd go with me to get pizza tonight?"

"In your car?"

"*Jah*. I'm too tired to hitch the horse and buggy."

"In that case, can we go to a fast food drive-through? I'm craving a burger and fries."

"Oh, and a nice, cold extra-large strawberry shake!"

Later, as they ate their takeout meals in the park, they didn't talk about anything more serious than old memories—bowling at the *Englisch* bowling alley, playing volleyball in the backyard, their father's rich singing voice and their mother's contagious laugh. Yet these lighthearted remembrances stirred a deep longing within Rachel's heart, and by the time they got home, she felt so emotionally and physically depleted she actually went to bed before Ivan did.

* * *

Long after he should have been asleep, Arden was mulling over how angry he'd gotten at Rachel. He'd suffered more than his fair share of derision before, but it had never provoked him the way it did when he thought Rachel was scorning him. To think, he'd gone so far as to devise a plan to force her out of her voluntary role in her brother's business! *What if Ivan does propose she relinquish her work in the business?* That might be just the impetus she needed to leave early. To go back to Toby. The thought made him shudder.

Whether she gets back together with him or not is beside the point. All I care about is reconciling with her. For as long or short of a time as Rachel had left in Serenity Ridge, Arden wanted their friendship to be like it was before... No, that wasn't the full truth. He wanted their relationship to be *better* than it was before: he wanted to admit to Rachel how he felt about her—which was unlike how he'd ever felt about any woman. But he could scarcely admit those feelings to himself, knowing he couldn't act on them. Not just because Rachel was *Englisch*, but because he could never get married, never have children. And since that was an impossibility, the best he could hope for was that the rest of his time with Rachel would be as good as their time together up until he'd acted like a genuine *dummkopf*.

Despite having a sleepless night, Arden woke early, milked the cow, ate and quickly got ready for church. He hoped to speak to Rachel before he and Ivan left, but her car wasn't in the driveway, and Ivan came out of the house alone.

"My *schweschder* made me wear it," he explained,

sheepishly pointing to the blue paper mask covering his face. "She's concerned people might get too close."

She was right. During the after-church lunch, so many people gathered around Ivan that he and Arden were among the last to leave. By the time they got to Ivan's house, Colin and Hadassah's buggy was in the driveway, but Rachel's car was not. "Ah, there's Hadassah and the *kinner*. She said they'd visit. She felt bad about forgetting my birthday," Ivan explained.

Hadassah had brought all four children, and the two eldest were pushing the younger two across the lawn in a wheelbarrow. Hadassah was sitting on the bench beneath the peach tree. How in the world had she managed to get down from the buggy? She appeared to have gained an inordinate amount of weight—even her hands were swollen.

"*Kumme* out of the sun, Hadassah. I'll bring you lemonade," Ivan said, and Arden helped her up the porch stairs.

Arden knew he should allow Ivan and Hadassah to visit in private, but he wanted to stay until Rachel returned. Fortunately, she pulled into the driveway a few minutes later. She slowly strolled across the lawn, stopping to talk to the children at length, and Arden couldn't guess whether she was dawdling in order to avoid him or Hadassah.

"Hi, Rachel," he said at the same time Ivan greeted her.

"Hello," she replied to neither of them in particular. "Hello, Hadassah."

"Hello," Hadassah said with a sniff, angling her face away from the sun.

"How are you feeling?" Rachel scrutinized her sister-in-law.

"We don't have allergies anymore, if that's what you're worried about."

"*Neh*, I can see that." She paused. "That dress is a fetching color on you, but—and this is a concern, not a criticism—your…your face looks very swollen."

Hadassah turned and looked Rachel up and down. "*Jah*, and yours is covered in fly bites."

To Arden's surprise, Rachel laughed. "Isn't it awful? I feel like a pincushion, but I haven't got any witch hazel. I remember when you told me how soothing that is."

Hadassah's expression softened noticeably. "Especially if it's kept in the fridge." She squeezed her eyes shut.

"Do you have a *koppweh*?" Rachel was concerned; Arden could tell.

"*Jah*. It's been raining so much that my eyes aren't used to the sun anymore. I keep seeing flashing lights."

Ivan stopped rocking the porch swing, as if he was picking up on Rachel's uneasiness, too.

"I don't want to alarm you, but I think you ought to see a *dok*—a midwife."

"I *am* seeing my midwife on Tuesday."

"I mean now. I think we should call an ambulance—"

"Don't be *lecherich*." Hadassah shifted to her side and pushed off the chair, panting. It took her three tries to get into a standing position, and when she was upright, she wobbled forward. Arden reflexively jumped up and steadied her by her elbow. "I came here to wish my brother-in-law a *hallich* birthday, not to be lectured about my health."

Before Hadassah could take another step, Rachel grabbed each side of the railing, barring her from leaving. Her voice was low but firm as she said, "Hadassah, you're a *wunderbaar mamm*, and I know how much you love all of your *kinner* as well as the two *bobblin* you're carrying. For their sakes, you must go to the hospital now. You have all the signs of a life-threatening condition. Please, I am begging you, please don't reject this advice just because it's coming from me. I know what it's like to lose my *mamm*—please don't allow that to happen to your *kinner*. Please don't leave my *bruder* a widower."

Hadassah grimaced. "Okay," she agreed, causing Arden to marvel at Rachel's gift of persuasion once again.

Rachel began issuing orders. "Ivan, get my phone from my purse and call nine-one-one. Tell them Hadassah has signs of preeclampsia, and it's a multiple pregnancy—how far along are you, Hadassah?" Rachel questioned before instructing Ivan what else to say. "Arden and I will help you inside, Hadassah. You need to lie on your left side."

"Can't you take her in your car?" Arden asked. "I think I can carry her if I need to. It will be faster."

"*Neh.* The paramedic will start an IV if necessary, and they'll be able to administer medication quicker than I'd be able to drive to the hospital."

They couldn't all get through the door at the same time, so Arden entered sideways, supporting Hadassah by himself. Before they were across the threshold, the children had assembled on the porch, apparently sensing the crisis.

"Is *Mamm* okay?" the oldest asked.

* * *

"She has a bad *koppweh*," Rachel calmly explained over her shoulder. "An ambulance is coming to take her to the hospital, where they're going to help her feel better. I'll get your *daed* and bring him to the hospital, too. I'd like you to stay here with your *onkel* Ivan and make sure he takes it easy. If you play a quiet board game with him, you may all have a glass of lemonade and a piece of cake."

The children expressed their agreement as Ivan provided an address to the dispatcher. As soon as Hadassah was situated on the bed, Rachel directed Arden to bring her the first aid kit from her car so she could take her sister-in-law's blood pressure. Silently praying as she worked, she'd just begun to inflate the cuff when the ambulance siren blared outside. Rachel stayed with Hadassah until the paramedic and EMT rolled her on a stretcher into the ambulance. "I'm going to go get Colin now, Hadassah. We'll see you very soon."

When she arrived at Colin's home, she immediately spotted him on the front porch with Eva and Ike Renno. Wasting no time with pleasantries, Rachel beckoned to him, urging, "Colin, you must *kumme* with me. Hadassah's been taken to the hospital by ambulance."

"We'll go get the *kinner*," Eva volunteered. "I'll stay with them here at the *haus* as long as needed."

As they drove, Rachel explained she suspected Hadassah had moderate to severe preeclampsia. "It's a very serious condition. They may induce labor, but most likely she'll need an emergency C-section." Rachel stole a sideways glance at Colin. A single tear ran down his cheek, like a crack in a stone wall. She reached over and squeezed his fist.

"Please, *Gott*, watch over my wife and our *bobblin*," he began praying. "Please, *Gott*, please."

He continued to pray, and Rachel silently echoed his prayers all the way to the hospital, where she dropped him off at the entrance and then went to park. By the time she got inside, Colin had already been taken to be with Hadassah, who was, indeed, undergoing an emergency C-section. It seemed like forever before Colin came to find Rachel in the waiting room. The blue scrubs were a stark contrast with his traditional Amish clothing, and his skin was sallow and his eyes were bloodshot. Rachel's heart pummeled her ribs.

"They made it. All three of them," he said. "My wife and two *seh*."

Rachel gasped, erupting into tears of joy. "*Denki*, Lord!" she uttered as Colin enveloped her.

"I'm sorry, Rachel," he said when he let her go, and at first she thought he meant for squeezing her so tightly. "*Mamm* and *Daed* put me in charge of watching over our *familye*. When you left, I…"

He couldn't finish his sentence, nor did he need to. Rachel understood; his anger about her leaving had been masking his disappointment in himself and concern for her. Similarly, his criticism of Ivan's business wasn't because he wanted to be in control; it was because he wanted to protect Ivan from failure. Until now, Rachel had only seen the austerity of Colin's actions, not the sense of fraternal responsibility behind his intentions, just as he'd only seen pride, not her desire to

help others, when she left to become a nurse. "I understand, Colin. I'm sorry, too."

After Eva and Ike came for the children and buggy,
Arden arranged for a taxi to take him and Ivan to the
hospital. They were deeply grateful to learn Hadassah
and the babies were all right. Since there was a limit
on the number of visitors who could enter the NICU
room, Rachel came out so Ivan and Arden could see
the babies once they'd washed their hands and put on
sterile gowns and gloves. Although Colin's mouth was
obscured by a paper mask, Arden could tell by the way
his eyes twinkled he was grinning.

"There's Jacob, and this is Daniel," he said, pointing
to where the babies slept in separate incubators.

"I know how that feels, *buwe*," Ivan joked about the
skinny oxygen tubes strapped to their noses.

"They're so tiny," Arden said. "But praise the Lord
they're okay."

"*Jah.* The *dokder* warned us about a host of condi-
tions they might face in the coming years because of
being born so early, but that's in the future. Just look at
them. They are alive. They are *Gott*'s gift to us."

As he listened to Colin's expression of fatherly love,
it occurred to Arden his own father must have felt the
same way when he was born. Arden hadn't ever really
thought about it before, but surely his dad knew his son
and daughter might suffer the same difficulties he himself had suffered. Yet that foreknowledge hadn't pre-
vented him from getting married, having children and
cherishing them as gifts from the Lord. *Why should I
let it stop me?* As Daniel waved his fist and began to

cry, Arden wiped his own eyes, overcome by a rush of emotion.

A nurse entered the room and chased Ivan and Arden out to the hall, where Rachel was conferring with a midwife. Arden overheard her giving the woman her cell phone number, and then she drove Ivan and Arden back to Ivan's home. She was so eager to go tell her nieces and nephews about their new baby brothers she didn't even turn off the car when she dropped the men off, so Arden didn't get a chance to apologize to her in private.

"Uh, Grace can *kumme* early in the morning to stay with Ivan if you want to go to the hospital," he said before shutting the door.

"*Denki*, I'd appreciate that," she replied in a tone that was neither unfriendly nor warm.

Grace seemed pleased for an excuse to visit with Ivan again, and the next morning she collected the eggs and milked the cow before Arden awoke. "I'll make breakfast at Ivan's *haus*, so Rachel gets sustenance since she probably didn't eat much yesterday."

Within an hour the four of them sat down to a hearty breakfast casserole, toast and coffee. "What happened to your face?" Grace asked Rachel. The small red spots Hadassah had pointed out the previous afternoon had grown into welts overnight.

"I took a walk in the woods Saturday. I was swarmed by black flies."

So that's where she was. Arden cringed, knowing he was the cause of both her emotional and physical irritation.

"We never got to hear your news the other night after Toby called. Was he part of what you were going to tell us?" Grace questioned.

"Toby? *Neh*. He was calling to…to reconcile." Rachel dabbed her mouth with a napkin.

"He's going to be your suitor again? I mean, to date you?" Grace pushed. "Was that your news?"

"*Neh*, he's not. My news was that I got accepted into the MSN program."

"That's *wunderbaar!*" Grace exclaimed. "Isn't that *wunderbaar*, Ivan and Arden?"

"*Jah*," they agreed, even though they both already knew. *But what's more* wunderbaar *is that Rachel's not getting back together with Toby*, Arden thought.

"*Denki*, but I've decided not to go," Rachel said.

"You're not going?" Grace sounded perplexed.

"*Neh*. I decided becoming a nurse practitioner wasn't…it wasn't really how the Lord was directing my steps. Anyway, I'd better get going. I'm sure Colin is itching to have me bring him a fresh change of clothing," Rachel said, pushing her chair away from the table. She hadn't taken more than three bites of her meal, but she felt too self-conscious in Arden's presence to eat. After experiencing an emergency like yesterday's, she was keenly aware of how petty it was to continue harboring ill will toward him.

The night before as she was reflecting on her conversation with Colin, it had occurred to Rachel that her brother might have meant to be helpful the day he suggested Rachel should go back to Boston and he could help Arden with the accounting. *I accused Colin of trying to take over Ivan's business, yet that's exactly what I did by covering the deficit. Even if my intentions were* gut *or I was pressed for time, I should have discussed it with Arden first.* She wanted to apologize, but she'd need privacy for that. Until then, she had a busy morning in front of her.

When she arrived at the hospital, Daniel and Jacob were asleep and Hadassah looked exhausted, too, so Rachel kept her visit short. Right before she left, Hadassah suggested Colin go change into the clean clothing Rachel had brought, so they could have a moment alone to chat.

No sooner did the door close behind him than Hadassah apologized. "I've been *baremlich* to you, Rachel, and I'm so sorry."

"It's okay. Some of that might have been from feeling ill or from hormones. During pregnancy, your estrogen and progesterone levels—" Rachel stopped. "Oops, sometimes I can't help myself."

"It's *gut* to share what you've learned. If you hadn't, I might not be alive now and neither would the *bobblin*," Hadassah said. "But it wasn't illness or hormones—I've acted this way toward you for over ten years. I was so… so hurt when you left. I know how demanding I can be, but instead of blaming myself for your leaving, I blamed you. I said it was *hochmut*."

Until now, it never dawned on Rachel that Hadassah thought she'd left because of *her*. "Hadassah, I didn't leave to get away from anything or anyone—I was going *toward* what I believed was *Gott*'s will for me at that time. If anything, you were one of the very people who made me so reluctant to go—I consider you to be my older sister. And older sisters are supposed to be bossy."

"Well, younger sisters are supposed to be spoiled." They were both laughing when Colin reentered the room.

"Did you ask her yet?" he questioned Hadassah.

When she shook her head, Colin said, "We, uh, we were wondering if you might be able to stay in Serenity Ridge a little longer than you planned? The staff here has suggested we line up a visiting nurse for the next couple of months to give us a hand…"

Rachel was stunned silent, so Hadassah interjected, "We promise not to pressure you to leave the *Englisch*."

Because she'd spoken about leaving the Amish so often, the notion of leaving the *Englisch* struck Rachel as funny, and she smiled. "I appreciate that, but I'd like a little time to think it over."

She didn't get any farther than the parking lot before she unequivocally knew what her decision would be. Leaning against her car, she dialed Meg's number to break the news to her. "You were right, Meg. I'm staying here," she blurted out without even saying hello first. "I'm returning to my Amish faith and lifestyle for *gut*."

"Oh, Rachel," her dear friend said with a sigh. "In your heart, you never really *left* the Amish for *gut*."

Although it was raining, as his sister prepared lunch, Arden waited outside on the porch in case a customer or delivery truck came by. Instead, it was Rachel's car that turned into the driveway. Arden shot across the lawn quicker than she could get out and close the door.

"Rachel, I owe you an apology," he began. As she looked up at him, wide-eyed, raindrops ran in tiny rivulets over the bright wheals on her face. "I—I—I am so ashamed of h-how I spoke to you yesterday. Everything I said was—was truer of me than of you. I was the one who m-made the m-mistake in the first place, but instead of being grateful for your help, I was rude and unkind. *Neh*—I was vicious."

She shook her head, and his hope for reconciliation crumbled until she said, "I forgive you, Arden, but I shouldn't have made that kind of decision without consulting you and Ivan. I can see now how patronizing my actions were. I'm very sorry."

"At least you were trying to be helpful. I was trying to be *hurt*ful, because…well, because *I* felt hurt." Although the rain was warm on his scalp and back, Arden shivered as he confessed, "I was also envious."

"Of what?"

"Of Toby."

"Why would you be envious of someone like *him*?"

Arden coughed, stalling. "He's so *schmaert* and—"

"And so are you! I meant it when I told you you're one of the smartest people I know."

"It isn't just that Toby's *schmaert*." A wet curl stuck to Arden's forehead, and he pushed it aside. "It's also th-that he symbolized something I thought I could never have."

"Such as?"

Arden couldn't face her. He looked over her shoulder, focusing on the trees in the distance. "M-marriage."

To whom? Rachel felt her insides melting like wax. Arden couldn't possibly mean *her*? "What's stopping you from getting married?"

"Nothing is now. But *I* w-was stopping myself before," Arden said. "I thought I should-shouldn't get married be-because my *kinner* w-would have the same problems I have."

"That's a possibility, but it's not an absolute. As you once said to me about my caring for Ivan, who would be better equipped to help that child than you?"

"I—I know that now. I figured it out when I saw how thrilled Colin was about his *bobblin*…"

Rachel giggled. "*Jah*, I didn't know he could still smile like that."

"Arden! Rachel! What are you doing out in the rain? Lunch is ready," Grace summoned them from the porch.

"We're coming." Rachel was disappointed their conversation had been interrupted, but she hoped they'd pick up where they left off once they had privacy again. When they got inside, they dried off and seated themselves at the table.

"I hope *rivel supp* is okay. *Mamm* and I were making it for Aquilla, so we figured we might as well make some for you, too," Grace said, and Ivan smiled politely.

After they'd thanked God for the meal, Rachel announced she had something for the other three to consider. "Grace, if your *mamm*'s health is stable and if Ivan and Arden agree to it, in a few days would you be willing to take over for me at the workshop on an ongoing basis—and check in on Ivan occasionally, too?"

Arden dropped the saltshaker right into his soup, spraying chowder everywhere. "You w-w-won't be wo-working at the shop anymore?"

"I don't know." Rachel handed him a spare napkin, but he made no attempt to mop up the spill. "Hadassah and Colin have asked me to help them for a couple of months once she and the *bobblin* are discharged. I'd like to do it, but Ivan won't be able to return to work for a while, and I don't want to leave the two of you in the lurch, which is why I thought Grace might be—"

"I'd be *hallich* to step in," Grace said.

Ivan simultaneously remarked, "Hadassah needs you more than we do."

"Jah," Arden agreed as he fished the saltshaker from his chowder. "You definitely should help Hadassah and the *bobblin.* It's a better use of your skills."

Rachel wasn't expecting everyone to be quite so enthusiastic about her relinquishing her position at the workshop. She had intended to tell them about her decision to be baptized into the Amish church, too, but what if they weren't receptive to the idea? Suddenly she could hardly fight back the tears. *"Gut,* it's settled then. If you'll excuse me, these clothes are wetter than I thought and I'm uncomfortable in them. I'll go change."

Upstairs she kicked off her shoes and curled into a ball, quietly weeping into a pillow. She understood that even if Arden had the smallest romantic inclination toward her, he wouldn't have been likely to express it. Not while she was still *Englisch.* But did he have to seem so happy she wouldn't be working with him any longer? *And to think, I dared hope when he was talking about wanting to get married, he might have had me in mind—which just goes to show how much* hochmut *I really do have!*

She didn't remember falling asleep, but when she awoke, she changed into her lavender dress, went into the bathroom and splashed cold water over her face in an attempt to soothe her swollen eyelids and ease the sting of her bug bites. Downstairs she found the table had been cleared, Grace was gone and Ivan was taking a nap. Instead of soup, she opted to have a glass of lemonade. As she was putting the pitcher back in the fridge, she noticed a brown paper bag with her name on it. Inside was a bottle of witch hazel and a note.

Rachel,
Hadassah needs you so I can't be selfish, but I
will miss you in the workshop. I wish you could
stay in Serenity Ridge forever.
Arden

Rachel hugged the bottle to her chest as she reread
the note three times. Then she put the witch hazel back
in the fridge and, with every ounce of restraint she could
muster, slowly picked her way around the puddles as
she walked toward the workshop. The sun was break-
ing through the clouds, and once again, Arden's eyes
mirrored the blue of the sky as he stepped outside. It
was as if he'd been waiting for her.

Glancing at the note in her hand, he said, "As you
know, I'm not very *gut* with words."

"This is the best *liebesbrief* I've ever received,"
Rachel gushed, and then she was immediately embarrassed she'd referred to it as a love letter. Was that
how Arden had intended it?

"*Gut*, because it's the best—and the only—*liebesbrief* I've ever written," he replied, and for now, that
was all he needed to say.

Epilogue

"Are you enjoying your work as a midwife's assistant?" Sadie Swarey asked Rachel.

"I can't think of anything else I'd rather do. It must have been *Gott*'s plan for me to be here when the twins were born—otherwise I might never have found out the *Englisch* midwives desperately needed an Amish person to work with them in Serenity Ridge."

"*Ach!* Speaking of twins, look—mine are getting in line for a third piece of *hochzich* cake." Sadie waved a finger at her two children, Elizabeth and David, across the church's gathering room. "*Gott segen*, Arden and Rachel."

After she walked away, Meg came over to where they were standing. "Rachel, you're glowing!" she remarked. "Oops, is that not allowed? Are compliments considered *hochmut*?"

Arden shrugged. "I hope not, because I keep telling Rachel the same thing."

"*Denki*," Rachel said to them both. "I'm so glad you took time off to be here, Meg."

"I wouldn't have missed it for anything. Although I feel a little out of place. Am I the only *Englischer* here?"

"*Neh.* The Jones *familye* is *Englisch.*"

"Did I hear you mentioning my name?" Chris Jones sauntered in their direction, grinning.

"*Jah.* Chris, meet Meg. She's my *gut* friend, and up until seven months ago, she was my roommate, too."

"Hello, Meg. If you'd like, I can stick close by. We'll be fish out of water together."

"That would be nice." A blush settled over Meg's face.

As the pair edged toward the dessert table, Arden teased Rachel. "I didn't realize matchmaking was one of your vices. You're worse than my *mamm.*"

"But wouldn't it be wonderful if Meg and Chris fell in love, got married and were as *hallich* together as Ivan and Grace, or as you and I are?"

"I doubt anyone else could ever be *this hallich.*" Arden discreetly nuzzled Rachel's ear as he whispered, "I didn't know I could be this *hallich,* myself."

"Just wait until we have *bobblin.* You'll be over-joyed."

"I can hardly wait. And I can't wait any longer for this, either," he said, before surreptitiously kissing his bride.

* * * * *

Don't miss the next book in Carrie Lighte's Amish of Serenity Ridge miniseries, coming in June!

Dear Reader,

During the many years I lived or vacationed in Maine, I never saw a moose in the wild. Frankly, after all I've heard and read about them, I'm not sure I'd *want* to see one except from the safety of my home or from my car as I drive in the opposite direction. Which isn't to suggest most moose are aggressive toward humans, because usually they're not, although they *can* be unpredictable and at thirty-five miles per hour, they'd definitely be able to outrun me.

However, since the moose is Maine's state animal, I'd be remiss if I didn't allow one to wander through the pages of my Serenity Ridge series. That's one of the wonderful things about writing and reading fiction— it allows us to encounter people, places and things we might not otherwise meet.

As for whether this is the last time Serenity Ridge's heroes and heroines cross paths with this great animal… I hope you'll read the next two books to find out!

Blessings,
Carrie Lighte

WE HOPE YOU ENJOYED
THIS BOOK FROM

LOVE INSPIRED
INSPIRATIONAL ROMANCE

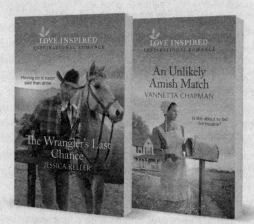

Uplifting stories of faith, forgiveness and hope.

Fall in love with stories where faith helps
guide you through life's challenges, and discover
the promise of a new beginning.

6 NEW BOOKS AVAILABLE EVERY MONTH!

4147

Get 4 FREE REWARDS!

We'll send you 2 FREE Books plus 2 FREE Mystery Gifts.

Love Inspired books feature uplifting stories where faith helps guide you through life's challenges and discover the promise of a new beginning.

FREE Value Over $20

YES! Please send me 2 FREE Love Inspired Romance novels and my 2 FREE mystery gifts (gifts are worth about $10 retail). After receiving them, if I don't wish to receive any more books, I can return the shipping statement marked "cancel." If I don't cancel, I will receive 6 brand-new novels every month and be billed just $5.24 each for the regular-print edition or $5.99 each for the larger-print edition in the U.S., or $5.74 each for the regular-print edition or $6.24 each for the larger-print edition in Canada. That's a savings of at least 13% off the cover price. It's quite a bargain! Shipping and handling is just 50¢ per book in the U.S. and $1.25 per book in Canada.* I understand that accepting the 2 free books and gifts places me under no obligation to buy anything. I can always return a shipment and cancel at any time. The free books and gifts are mine to keep no matter what I decide.

Choose one: ☐ **Love Inspired Romance Regular-Print** (105/305 IDN GNWC)   ☐ **Love Inspired Romance Larger-Print** (122/322 IDN GNWC)

Name (please print)

Address   Apt. #

City   State/Province   Zip/Postal Code

Mail to the **Reader Service:**
IN U.S.A.: P.O. Box 1341, Buffalo, NY 14240-8531
IN CANADA: P.O. Box 603, Fort Erie, Ontario L2A 5X3

Want to try 2 free books from another series! Call 1-800-873-8635 or visit www.ReaderService.com.

*Terms and prices subject to change without notice. Prices do not include sales taxes, which will be charged (if applicable) based on your state or country of residence. Canadian residents will be charged applicable taxes. Offer not valid in Quebec. This offer is limited to one order per household. Books received may not be as shown. Not valid for current subscribers to Love Inspired Romance books. All orders subject to approval. Credit or debit balances in a customer's account(s) may be offset by any other outstanding balance owed by or to the customer. Please allow 4 to 6 weeks for delivery. Offer available while quantities last.

Your Privacy—The Reader Service is committed to protecting your privacy. Our Privacy Policy is available online at www.ReaderService.com or upon request from the Reader Service. We make a portion of our mailing list available to reputable third parties that offer products we believe may interest you. If you prefer that we not exchange your name with third parties, or if you wish to clarify or modify your communication preferences, please visit us at www.ReaderService.com/consumerchoice or write to us at Reader Service Preference Service, P.O. Box 9062, Buffalo, NY 14240-9062. Include your complete name and address.

LI20R

The Wrangler's Last Chance
JESSICA KELLER

Their Wander Canyon Wish
ALLIE PLEITER

"Look, Mommy!" Sawyer ran over to them. A grubby, slimy—and very dead—worm rested in the palm of his hand.

"Ew."

At her disgust, Sawyer showed the prize to Evan. "Good find. He looks like he's dead, though, so you'd better give him a proper burial."

"Yeah!" Sawyer hurried over to the patch of dirt. He plopped the worm onto the sidewalk and told it to "stay" just like he would Belay. That made both of them laugh. Then he used one of the sticks as a shovel and began digging a hole.

"He's like a cat, always bringing me dead animals as gifts. I'm surprised he doesn't leave them for me on the doorstep."

Evan chuckled while waving toward the parking lot. She turned to see his brother and Mackenzie walking to their vehicle.

"Do you guys want to come out to Wilder Ranch for lunch? I'm sure they wouldn't mind two more. It's a happy sort of chaos there with all of the kids."

Addie's heart constricted at the offer. No doubt Sawyer would love it. She wanted exactly what Evan was offering, but all of that was off-limits for her. She couldn't allow herself any more access into Evan's world or vice versa.

"We can't, but thanks. I've got to get Sawyer down for a nap." Addie wasn't about to attempt attending a meeting with a tired Sawyer, and she didn't have anywhere else in town for him to go.

Evan's face morphed from relaxed to taut, but he didn't press further. "Right. Okay. I guess I'll see you later then." After saying goodbye to Sawyer, he caught up with Jace and Mackenzie in the parking lot.

A momentary flash of loss ached in Addie's chest. A few days in Evan's presence and he was already showing her how different things could have been. It was like there was a life out there that she'd missed by taking the wrong path. It was shiny and warm and so, so out of reach.

And the worst of it was, until Evan, she hadn't realized just how much she was missing.

Don't miss
Her Hidden Hope *by Jill Lynn,*
available May 2020 wherever
Love Inspired books and ebooks are sold.

LoveInspired.com

LIEXP0420

Addie kept monopolizing Evan's time. First at the B and B—though she could hardly blame herself for that. He was the one who'd insisted on helping her out. And now again at church. Surely he had better places to be than with her.

"Do you need to go?" she asked Evan. "Sorry I kept you so long."

"I'm not in a rush. I might pop out to Wilder Ranch for lunch with Jace and Mackenzie. After that I have to…" Evan groaned.

"Run into a burning building? Perform brain surgery? Teach a sewing class?"

Humor momentarily flashed across his features. "Go to a meeting for Old Westbend Weekend."

What? So much for some Evan-free time to pull herself back together. "I'm going to that, but I didn't realize you were. The B and B is one of the sponsors for the weekend." Addie had used her entire limited advertising budget for the three-day event.

"I thought my brother might block for me today. Instead he totally kicked me under the bus as it roared by. He caught Bill's attention and volunteered me for the hero thing." The pure torment on Evan's face was almost comical. "I want to back out of it, but Bill played the 'it's for the kids' card, and now I think I'm trapped."

COMING NEXT MONTH FROM
Love Inspired

Available April 21, 2020

A SUMMER AMISH COURTSHIP
by Emma Miller
With her son's misbehavior interrupting classes, Amish widow Abigail Stoltz must join forces with the schoolmaster, Ethan Miller. But as Ethan tutors little Jamie, Abigail can't help but feel drawn to him...even as her son tries to push them apart. Can they find a way to become a forever family?

AMISH RECKONING
by Jocelyn McClay
A new client is just what Gail Lapp's horse transportation business needs to survive. But as the single mom works with Amish horse trader Samuel Schrock, she's pulled back into the world she left behind. And returning to her Amish life isn't possible if she wants to keep her secrets...

THE PRODIGAL COWBOY
Mercy Ranch • by Brenda Minton
After their daughter's adoptive mom passes away and names Colt West and Holly Carter as guardians, Colt's determined to show Holly he isn't the unreliable bachelor she once knew. But as they care for their little girl together, can the cowboy prove he'd make the perfect father...and husband?

HER HIDDEN HOPE
Colorado Grooms • by Jill Lynn
Intent on reopening a local bed-and-breakfast, Addie Ricci sank all her savings into the project—and now the single mother's in over her head. But her high school sweetheart's back in town and happy to lend a hand. Will Addie's long-kept secret stand in the way of their second chance?

WINNING BACK HER HEART
Wander Canyon • by Allie Pleiter
When his ex-girlfriend returns to town and hires him to overhaul her family's general store, contractor Bo Carter's determined to keep an emotional distance. But to convince her old boss she's home for good, Toni Redding needs another favor—a pretend romance. Can they keep their fake love from turning real?

AN ALASKAN TWIN SURPRISE
Home to Owl Creek • by Belle Calhoune
The last person Gabriel Lawson expects to find in town is Rachel Marshall—especially with twin toddlers in tow. Gabriel refuses to risk his heart again on the woman who once left him at the altar years ago. But can they overcome their past to consider a future?